The
CHILD
SNATCHER

The
CHILD
SNATCHER

Aria Johnson

INFINITE WORDS

P.O. Box 6505
Largo, MD 20792
www.simonandschuster.com

This book is a work of fiction. Names, characters, places and incidents are products of the author's imagination or are used fictitiously. Any resemblance to actual events or locales or persons, living or dead, is entirely coincidental.

© 2016 by Aria Johnson

ISBN 978-1-59309-696-0
ISBN 978-1-5011-1914-9 (ebook)
LCCN 2016948654

First Infinite Words trade paperback edition October 2016

Cover design: www.mariondesigns.com
Cover photograph: © Keith Saunders/Keith Saunders Photos
Book design: Red Herring Design, Inc.

10 9 8 7 6 5 4 3 2 1

Manufactured in the United States of America

For information regarding special discounts for bulk purchases, please contact Simon & Schuster Special Sales at 1-866-506-1949 or business@simonandschuster.com

The Simon & Schuster Speakers Bureau can bring authors to your live event. For more information or to book an event, contact the Simon & Schuster Speakers Bureau at 1-866-248-3049 or visit our website at www.simonspeakers.com.

For Carl Edward Johnson

Chapter 1

I arrived at work wearing concealer under my eyes, a dab of blush on my cheeks, and my lips were glossed with a cheerful raspberry tint. I rarely bothered with makeup, but I hoped the added color would hide the fact that I'd cried myself to sleep last night.

Veronica ambled toward my desk, carrying a cup of coffee. She was a sturdy woman in her seventies, one of the five members of the horticulture department that I supervised. She wore the required uniform: a green shirt and khaki-colored slacks, covered with a protective smock. Having a position of management, I was allowed to wear regular clothes, but I would have loved the convenience of a uniform.

"You look pretty, Claire. Hot lunch date?" Veronica inquired, her dark eyes twinkling with mischief.

"Wouldn't that be nice? But it's unlikely that I'll ever get a date if I don't start putting a little more effort into my appearance." My attempt at lightheartedness fell flat and my voice came out sounding as exhausted as I felt.

She placed the coffee on my desk. "It's good and strong. Should help wake you up," she added knowingly as she stared into my tired eyes.

No amount of makeup could disguise a beleaguered spirit, I surmised as I guzzled the mud-colored elixir as if it had healing properties.

"By the way, how's Brandon making out?" Veronica folded her arms as if bracing herself for my latest tale of woe.

Brandon was a perpetually unhappy and hostile young man, and she was aware that only two days ago, he had kicked the closet door of his bedroom with an unflagging fury, stopping only when his sneaker had become embedded in the wood. The week before that, while sitting at the breakfast table eating cereal, he'd quietly threatened to poison the neighbor's dog if it didn't stop barking so much.

It was obvious by the way Veronica's lips were pursed together that she was struggling against the urge to chastise me for allowing Brandon to "walk all over me," as she often put it.

Despite our age difference, Veronica was my closest friend and confidante on the job. Stubbornly refusing to retire, the gutsy seventy-two-year-old had sued for age discrimination—and won—when the head honchos had tried to downsize her position.

Although she knew much more about plant life than I did, my master's degree in horticulture outranked her high school diploma and I'd been her supervisor for the past seven years. At least on paper I was. In reality, Veronica was as knowledgeable as a doctorate botanist when it came to the art of garden cultivation.

Possessing a nurturing spirit, she often mothered me. Believing I'd been dealt a bad hand in life, she fussed over me, making my coffee every morning and often bringing me home-cooked food when she thought I was getting too thin. She also served as my armchair therapist and a trusted adviser when it came to matters concerning my brooding—and at times violent—socially awkward son.

"Brandon is fine," I said in a sharp tone that warned her to back off. "Really, he's fine," I added more gently when I noticed a trace of hurt flit across her face.

Actually, Brandon was anything but fine. Before going to bed last night, I'd stood outside his bedroom door with a fist poised to knock as I listened to him sobbing and muttering mournfully, "Why? Why'd she do this to me? I did everything for her."

In addition to his father's abandonment, this was the second major heartbreak of my son's life. I didn't have the answer to why his so-called girlfriend had broken up with him, and since any words of comfort from me would further enrage him, I slunk away from his door, feeling helpless.

As Veronica hovered nearby, I eyed my computer monitor, pretending to be immersed in the blur of words and numbers on the screen while my mind wandered to last night. I'd had a hard time getting to sleep and repeatedly sprang upright with my heart racing, thinking I'd heard a thump or thud. "You okay, Brandon?" I had yelled from my bedroom. Of course, my question had been met with silence. My son was much too inconsiderate to bother putting my mind at ease with a response.

After being startled by an odd humming noise, I threw off the covers and crept down the hall toward Brandon's room, stopping short outside his door. A hand covered my mouth and I blinked back tears as I listened to the mournful sound of my son sobbing. From previous experiences, I knew it wouldn't be long before his pitiful cries escalated to a one-sided tirade that culminated in either the shattering of glass or the crash of a waste bin being kicked across the room.

Noticing that I had drifted off in thought, Veronica gave my shoulder an understanding squeeze and ambled over to a shipment of fertilizer and potted hydrangea, allowing me to sink even deeper into my inner world.

As my thoughts hurtled back to last night, I recalled how I'd tossed and turned and quietly wept, and then finally slipped into a fitful sleep.

Although Brandon had never indicated that he wished to seriously harm anyone, a part of me was terrified that one day he would. His rage fully possessed him at times.

If my son were a girl, I imagined he would have been a cutter. Or an anorexic. Or both. It seemed to me that emotionally troubled girls tended to provide warning signs before they did something terrible. But boys didn't give any glaring indicators that they were about to go on a shooting rampage at their high school. Like Brandon, the brooding behavior of those kids who massacred their classmates had been ongoing for such a long time, it was considered more of a personality defect than a mental health issue.

Though he still behaved like a bratty kid, Brandon was practically grown. At twenty years old, he no longer had to follow my orders, and I couldn't force him to get counseling for his mood swings that went from depression to rage.

During Brandon's high school years when he had changed from a quietly sullen boy to a raging teen that was verbally abusive to neighbors, teachers, and even me, I'd hustled him off to a series of psychologists. I was repeatedly told there was nothing clinically wrong with him. He exhibited a behavioral problem known as oppositional defiant disorder, which didn't require medication. The clinicians informed me that Brandon's disorder involved a variety of genetic and environmental factors. Mainly environmental factors, insisted one of his therapists, and she seemed to point a finger at me. The mother was always to blame.

It was recommended that Brandon attend family therapy with both parents, but my ex-husband, Howard, refused to participate.

Brandon's behavior at those sessions had been embarrassing. He openly sulked, defiantly rested his cruddy boots on top of the therapist's pristine coffee table, and glared at both the therapist and me, responding to all questions with seething sarcasm. So, we stopped going.

But he had gotten worse, and there was no denying that my son needed some kind of treatment. If he agreed to go, I'd be willing to sit through the agonizing sessions alongside him with a pained smile plastered on my face. I'd do whatever it took to usher my child into adulthood as a happy, self-sufficient, and well-adjusted human being.

It would have been nice to have the hot lunch date that Veronica had hinted at, but it was impossible for me to enjoy any kind of pleasure when I felt like such a failure as a mom. Until Brandon became a functioning adult and at peace with himself, any joy that life possibly held for me was temporarily on hold.

It was a habit to check on Brandon as soon as I woke up each day. This morning when I quietly cracked open his door, I found his room in its normal messy state with an overflowing trash bin, old pizza boxes, and piles of dirty laundry. I felt immense relief that there were no shards of broken glass. No toppled furniture. No recent holes in the wall.

My deeply troubled man-child was sleeping soundly with an expression so blissful and angelic, I'd been tempted to forge a path through all the junk on the floor and steal a quick kiss on his cheek.

But I hadn't. No point in taking the risk of disturbing him from the peaceful slumber that protected him from his waking belief that he was a *fucktard*, a *dipshit*, an *asshat*, and any number of the self-bashing slurs that he routinely hurled at himself...aloud.

Being Brandon's mother should have aged me. Should have grayed my hair and given me wrinkles, yet there were no outward signs of aging. At forty-two, I was surprisingly youthful considering all I'd been through. To my amazement, I was often mistaken for my son's sister.

Imagining that the decline and erosion were taking place on the inside, I grimaced at the notion of having vital organs that were diseased and rapidly failing, one-by-one. In the midst of pondering the condition of my internal organs, Veronica reappeared at my desk. She ran a hand over her close-cropped, gray hair and sighed as she took a seat beside my desk.

"You can tell me to butt out, but it wouldn't be right if I didn't at least try to talk some sense into you. I realize how protective you are of Brandon, and this is a touchy subject, but..." Veronica paused.

I groaned inwardly, sensing that she was gearing up to lecture me about my culpability in the way Brandon had turned out.

It briefly occurred to me to fabricate a story and tell her that Howard had offered our son a position at his real estate firm. For good measure, I could add that Brandon was so enthused, he'd signed up for an online real estate course. But what would have been the point? Veronica would have seen right through my lies, and Brandon would still be jobless, sequestered in his bedroom, trolling the Internet, and playing video games.

I could have simply told her to mind her own business, but she meant well and I didn't want to be disrespectful.

She cleared her throat. "Claire, you have to face the fact that you're not doing Brandon any favors by coddling him. In fact, you're enabling his behavior."

"You're being overly dramatic, making it sound as if Brandon has a drug problem," I said defensively.

"You know what I mean. To allow a practically grown man to lie around, doing nothing, is setting him up for failure later in life. He's never going to learn to take care of himself if you make life easy for him."

"He needs time to—"

Veronica held up a hand. "He dropped out of college well over a year ago. He's not going to amount to much if he continues down the path he's on."

I scowled in aggravation. "What path? You make it sound as if he's involved in criminal activity."

"Brandon needs tough love and if you don't make him get off his butt and get a job, you're going to be taking care of your grown son for the rest of your life."

I sighed wearily. "You have no idea the amount of strength it takes to keep pushing someone who refuses to budge."

"You're the mother—so act like it. Make Brandon get off his lazy tail and do something worthwhile with his life."

"Some kids mature late in life. I'm sure he'll figure things out in his own time." My lack of sleep was taking a toll and I didn't have the strength to defend myself against Veronica's badgering.

"Are you saying you're willing to put up with his outbursts indefinitely? Do you mean to tell me that you're going to allow a twenty-year-old *man* to keep having tantrums and bashing holes in your walls...along with all of his other shenanigans?"

I made a mental note to stop sharing my personal problems with Veronica. Had I not disclosed so many details of Brandon's behavior, I wouldn't have to put up with her righteous indignation.

"Brandon has emotional issues," I said somberly and then gave a shrug of defeat.

"Then, he should be getting treatment."

"He's not psychotic. He's merely high-strung. Always has been... you know that."

"All I know is that you make a lot of excuses for him, and if he's not pointed in the right direction soon, he's going to end up a forty-year-old ne'er-do-well."

Ne'er-do-well. I cringed at her archaic choice of words. *Loser* would have sufficed just fine.

I massaged my temple. "I'm tired of fighting with him. I give up. I simply don't care anymore." But the pitiful whine that slipped into my voice was a dead giveaway—a sign that I *did* care. I cared so much I could feel a kind of pressure in the center of my chest, and the hand that had been massaging my temple moved down to my chest, and began rubbing circularly.

"Are you okay?" Veronica asked.

"Heartburn," I mumbled, pulling open my desk drawer and seizing a container of Tums.

Veronica gripped the handle of the cart she used to transport plants and pushed it toward the door. "Do you need anything?" she asked, looking over her shoulder at me with a softened expression.

I shook my head. "No, I'm fine."

She nodded before shuffling off to the greenhouse to tend to the flowers and foliage in there.

With Veronica out of my hair for the next hour or so, I returned my attention to the computer screen, prepared to spend the next few hours writing the dreaded biannual job evaluations for the seven horticulturists—including Veronica—whose jobs included maintaining the grounds, creating eye-catching floral designs, and overseeing the on-site organic composting program at the small children's zoo where I was employed as the Director of Horticulture.

It was a lofty title that didn't match my laughably small salary. Although I deserved and certainly could have used more money, especially since Howard had stopped paying child support the moment he'd discovered that Brandon had dropped out of college, I remained in my position because of my love of greenery.

Though I seldom got the opportunity to actually work with the plants that my department nurtured, I experienced the wonderful sensation of having my hands in soil more at home than at work. I had a stunning flower garden in my front yard that was my pride and joy. Simply being around flowers and enjoying their beauty allowed me to forget my troubles, bringing peace and sanity to my chaotic world.

I labored over the evaluations, working straight through lunch, and waving away Veronica's offer to share her home-cooked pot roast. I was determined to finish, but had to pull myself away from the tedious work to attend a management meeting that was so boring, it was a struggle to stay awake.

After the meeting, I called Brandon and asked what he wanted for dinner.

"Not hungry," he said in the typical monotone he spoke in whenever he wasn't bellowing about how much his life sucked.

"You'll be hungry later," I reminded him in a patient tone. "I could stop at Taco Bell or Domino's. Do you want...Mexican or pizza, hon?"

"I don't care," he muttered irritably. "Get whatever you want, Mom." He disconnected the call before I could come up with other food suggestions.

Chapter 2

Brandon called an hour later while I was stuck in crawling traffic.

"Are you on your way home?"

"I'm actually on my way to Taco Bell. Why?"

"We haven't had Thai food in a while. Would you mind picking up something from House of Siam?" His tone was surprisingly polite and upbeat.

House of Siam was on the other side of town, but I didn't mind going out of my way because there was something in Brandon's tone that filled me with hope. Maybe he would make an effort to get himself together and stop brooding over that vile girl who'd broken his heart. God only knew what he'd seen in such an unsavory character in the first place.

In the midst of bumper-to-bumper traffic, I managed to make a U-turn and steered the car in the opposite direction. My mind wandered to Brandon's laptop. I gripped the steering as I recalled how my son would sit and stare at his screensaver, an image of a girl named Ava that he'd met in a porn chat room.

There was nothing cute about Ava. She looked perpetually pissed-off with mean, squinty eyes, a hawk nose, and a turned-down mouth.

Tattoos splattered her neck and shoulders, and her stringy hair was streaked with all sorts of colors. Ava probably wasn't even her real name, but one of numerous Internet monikers.

My lips puckered in distaste. Although I'd never met her personally, I could tell by her expression—the tight way she held her mouth—that she wasn't very nice. And some of the unpleasant things Brandon told me she'd said after she dumped him for a *girl* proved that she was a cruel person.

Why don't you grow some balls and stop acting like a bitch? What're you, a stalker? My new girlfriend's more man than you'll ever be and she's gonna kick your ass if you keep calling and harassing me.

Brandon was much better off without that atrocious girl and I hoped he realized it. If only he'd take my advice and enroll in our area's community college, he could meet nice girls who weren't covered in tattoos. I was sure he'd be a happier person if only he'd stay out of chat rooms, get out of the house, and start mingling with young people who didn't hide behind screen names and who actually had goals in life.

Then again, maybe sitting in a structured class environment wasn't the right fit for him. Perhaps he needed to do something creative and use his hands. Culinary school, maybe? It was an idea worth looking into since part of Brandon's grievances over the breakup was that he'd done all the cooking and cleaning during the short three weeks he'd shared an apartment with Ava.

I'd never known my son to be interested in puttering around the kitchen or in keeping things tidy, and I wondered if the cooking thing was a hidden talent he'd inadvertently stumbled upon out of necessity.

It didn't matter what profession he chose, I simply wanted him to be self-sufficient and happy with himself.

I blamed Howard for all of Brandon's problems. It was infuriating the way he doted on his three children from his current marriage while ignoring his firstborn. We lived in a small town and it was quite common to bump into Howard and his new family. He'd nod his head at Brandon and sometimes he asked how he was doing, but basically, he acted as if he didn't know Brandon very well. And in truth, he didn't. He didn't want to.

As I approached my home, I was surprised to see a beat-up old Honda tearing away from the curb in front of our house. With no concern for the speed limit, the car roared down our quiet residential street. A fleeting glimpse of the driver caused me to recoil. *Ava.* Despite never being formally introduced to her, I'd recognize her sour expression and dramatic hair anywhere.

With a sense of urgency, I pushed down on the gas pedal and zipped into our driveway, rolling over my flower garden and prized azaleas as I parked haphazardly. Clutching the handles of the shopping bag filled with Thai food, I hurried inside, pretty certain that Ava had said or done something to ruin Brandon's good mood.

I entered the house not knowing what to expect. Another hole in the wall? Smashed dishes? Would he be curled in a fetal knot, sobbing inconsolably?

To my amazement, Brandon seemed untroubled by Ava's visit. In fact, he seemed jubilant, his lips stretching back into a big grin when he spotted the bag of Thai food. It was a boyish, unrestrained smile that I rarely saw anymore, and it warmed my heart. Maybe my son had turned a corner emotionally and was ready to climb out of the doldrums and move forward with his life.

"Are you okay, Brandon?" I asked cautiously. Although I was curious about Ava's visit, I didn't want to upset him by bringing up her name.

"I'm great, Mom. Ava came by. She thinks we should try to work through our issues and maybe get back together." His smile reappeared, and this time it was lopsided and goofy.

I groaned inwardly as I busied myself with setting the table. I wondered how Ava's lesbian lover felt about a possible reconciliation between her girlfriend and my son. Of course I didn't verbalize my thoughts. Brandon was too fragile for me to open up that can of worms.

I cut an eye at Brandon and flinched. It both pained and infuriated me to witness the gullible smile on his face.

"How could you even consider getting involved with that girl, again when she was so cruel to you?" I asked.

"She has her ways, but Ava's okay once you get to know her."

"I don't want to know her, and I'd appreciate it if you didn't invite her here."

"She had a rough life, Mom. The only family she had was an uncle who only cared about booze. She realizes that she's damaged, and she wants to change. We're back together, and we're both going to put in the effort to make the relationship work this time."

Questioning his sanity, I stared unblinkingly at Brandon. "That girl is toxic! She'll turn on you at the drop of a dime."

"No, she won't. We both agreed that we should settle down and start a family," he explained, his face morphing into another foolish expression. My boy was so naïve, it both astonished and shamed me.

"Are you kidding? That is the most ridiculous..." My voice trailed off. There weren't any words in the English language to adequately express my shock and disdain, and so I began making inarticulate, random sounds while rolling my eyes heavenward.

"She said she was ovulating, and so we, uh, you know..." His face flushed and he dropped his gaze.

It took a few moments for his words to sink in. "You had sex with that awful girl...right here in our home?" I turned up my nose like I suddenly smelled a foul odor.

"Yeah, but we weren't, like, downstairs on the couch or anything. We were in the privacy of my bedroom."

"This is not a sleazy hotel, Brandon. It's our home, and that wayward girl is not welcome here. Are we clear on that?"

His expression darkened and became taut with indignation, and then he gave me a cocky half-smile. Instead of answering, he jutted his chin and crossed his arms defiantly. *This is my house, too,* his body language said.

"Why do you always have to be such a bitch, Mom?" Before I had time to react to the disrespectful language, he picked up the bag of Thai food and hurled it against the wall, causing an explosion of beef, noodles, and red curry sauce.

Brandon kicked the overturned bag for good measure and then stormed out of the kitchen and stomped up the stairs.

I gawked at the disaster of red and green guck that oozed down the wall and puddled on the floor. Sinking into a kitchen chair, I wondered where in the world to begin cleaning up the mess. I felt world weary and old. I needed a vacation. No, I needed to just pick up and move in the dead of the night. Somewhere far, far away from my troubled son.

In the morning, before I left for work, I found Brandon seated at the kitchen table eating cereal and talking on the phone. He was eerily calm as he spoke softly—to Ava, no doubt.

Even though he'd behaved like a monster last night, I couldn't help the rush of love I felt for him. As I poured myself a glass of orange juice, I rustled his hair. God, I loved his curly, brown hair. He looked up at me with the sweetest smile, and I could feel my heart melt. But I wondered how long his serene mood would last. A full day? Or would he be on another destructive rampage when I returned home from work tonight?

My son had turned into a real-life Dr. Jekyll and Mr. Hyde, and I had to face the fact that despite what the doctors had said in the past, Brandon's mood swings were not going to level out on their own. He needed treatment and medication.

At work, my desk and computer was in the midst of a highly trafficked area where many of the department supplies were kept. It was more like a junky multipurpose room than an office. Most days, my work area resembled Grand Central Station with my staff of seven streaming in and out continuously throughout the day.

I waited until they'd all cleared out and had gone to work on the zoo grounds before I called Howard. I dreaded talking with my ex, but after Brandon's latest meltdown, I felt I had no choice but to reach out to his father and discuss having him placed in a psychiatric facility on a seventy-two-hour hold.

Howard's secretary placed me on hold for an unreasonably long time and when he finally picked up, it was apparent that I'd caught him at a bad time. "What can I do for you, Claire?" he asked gruffly.

I gave him a quick summary of Brandon's depression that was followed by violent outbursts. I expressed concern about his involvement with a sleazy girl whom I left unnamed. I was too embarrassed to mention Brandon's sudden and irrational desire to father a child with the revolting girl. I'd save that outlandish tidbit for the psychiatrist once we got Brandon the help he needed.

"Brandon's an adult; don't you think it's time to cut the apron strings?"

"His age doesn't matter. As his parents, we have to make an effort to get him diagnosed."

"Let me get this straight; you want to have him committed because he had sex with a girl you don't approve of?" Howard asked with a spiteful chuckle.

"It's more than that. His behavior has gotten more and more erratic lately, and I'm worried sick about him. One moment he's calm and pleasant, and the next, he's brooding. The brooding escalates to violent outbursts. I honestly believe he's bipolar. But I can't get him properly diagnosed because he refuses to see a psychiatrist."

"Can't say I blame him on the shrink thing. When he was little, you thought he had ADHD. During his teen years, you labeled him with every mental illness in the book. He's been seen by a battery of neurologists, child psychologists, and shrinks, and they all said there's nothing wrong with the kid other than his bratty disposition. He's been mean-spirited from day one."

"I suppose the apple doesn't fall far from the tree, then," I muttered with a snort.

"My point is...the kid knows how to work you. He always has, Claire."

"He doesn't *work* me. I don't think he can help the way he acts. There's something wrong with his brain. His symptoms suggest—"

Howard cut me off with a scoffing sound. "You've been making up symptoms since he was little. Makes me wonder if *you're* the nutjob. It's possible that you suffer from Munchausen syndrome."

"That's a horrible thing to say."

"There's nothing wrong with Brandon other than being lazy, spoiled, and too dependent on his mother. He needs to toughen up. It's as simple as that. If you want my advice, I think you should drop him off at an Army recruitment office. Let the military make a man out of him. I don't know what else to recommend for the kid."

There was finality in Howard's tone, and I could picture him checking his watch. His mind, already off Brandon, had moved on to business meetings, contracts, and closing deals.

There was a brief but awkward silence as my mind raced, trying to think of something that would reel Howard in and get him as emotionally involved with Brandon's issues as I was.

"Could you talk to him, Howard? Man-to-man. And maybe get to the bottom of what's bugging him? Take him to a ballgame or wrestling match. It wouldn't kill you to spend some father-and-son time with him."

I could sense Howard bristling at my suggestion. "The kid won't open up to me," he said tonelessly.

"Perhaps he'd be more forthcoming if you didn't act like he was a random stranger, constantly referring to him as *the kid* and flaunting your new family in his face," I said bitterly. I'd intended to keep my voice calm and I had promised myself that I wouldn't bring up Howard's current wife and children, but his aloofness and obvious disconnect with our son was infuriating.

"Claire, we've had this same conversation a million times, and I'm telling you for the millionth time that I don't have the time or patience for an oversized brat with a perpetually pissed-off attitude. That kid whines and complains more than my five-year-old twin girls. My eight-year-old son is more adult-like than Brandon," Howard bragged. His words stung badly.

From what I'd observed in passing, Howard's kids seemed polite and well adjusted, which pissed me off in a major way.

"If it were up to me," Howard continued, "I'd force the kid to man-up by releasing him into the wild and letting him fend for himself. I'd deal with his tantrums by beating his ass with a bag of oranges—" Howard laughed midsentence. "I'd prefer to use a bag of locks, but oranges don't leave any marks."

I flinched as if he'd struck me. I hadn't expected such an acerbic reply from Howard, such a glaring admission of his utter loathing for his own flesh and blood. "You're a despicable human being, and I was delusional to even hope you'd pretend to give a damn about your son," I lashed out.

Howard laughed cruelly. "You created that monster—not me. You're the one who didn't believe in discipline. It used to boggle my mind the way you would ask him if he needed a hug whenever he screamed at the top of his lungs for no reason, or when he spitefully kicked his blocks over or hurled his sippy cup against the wall. After our divorce was final, I ran as fast as I could from both of you kooks. I took care of my financial responsibilities and never missed a child support payment, but no judge in the world could force me to spend quality time with that obnoxious brat. To this day, I regret siring that kid."

Howard's cruel words drew another gasp from me and left me speechless.

"Listen, I'm running late for a meeting. I have to go, but before I hang up, I want to stress that Brandon is not a child anymore, nor is he my problem. My family life is calm and orderly and I deeply resent being dragged into the chaos that you created. So do me a favor and lose my number."

The phone went dead and I stared at it blankly for a few seconds and then my eyes began to water. It was amazing that after all these years, Howard still had the ability to cause me tremendous emotional pain. It didn't matter how he felt about me, but his contempt for Brandon hurt me to my core.

I heard a commotion out in the corridor and quickly wiped my eyes. I picked up a copy of *Horticulture* magazine and began thumbing through it.

Lugging a cart that was laden with bags of mulch and potted plants, Veronica returned to the office huffing and puffing and wiping perspiration from her forehead.

"Whew! All that bending and squatting is getting to the old girl. I'm going to have to soak in a tub of Epsom salt when I get home," she exclaimed, grimacing as she rubbed her left hip.

Although the rest of the staff were still outdoors shoveling, planting, trimming hedges, and doing other miscellaneous tasks that were part of the upkeep of the zoo's grounds, Veronica was ready to wind down. She had a doctor's note that exempted her from doing manual labor for more than three hours a day.

"Want some tea?" she inquired, groping through the cabinet above the microwave.

"No thanks." I kept my eyes down, pretending to be focused on an article in the magazine.

"Is everything all right?" she asked. She had a sixth sense when it came to my troubled home life.

"Yes, I'm fine."

"No, you're not. You're letting that boy of yours drive you batty. You need to get out of the house more often. It's not healthy being cooped up inside with all that negativity." She went quiet as she pondered the tea choices.

My eyes flitted back to the article I was pretending to read.

"Why don't you join me at my center after work today?" she asked.

Appalled, I stared at her with a frown. "No offense, but I don't want to go to a senior center?"

"It's a family center...people of all ages attend. It's Latin night and I'm gonna learn how to salsa." Forgetting about her alleged bad hip, Veronica broke into a few dance moves and was surprisingly rhythmic.

"I can't," I said, laughing. "Not with my two left feet."

"It's not a competition; it's a class and the instructor is really patient. You only live once, so why not try something new," she cajoled.

Veronica was thirty years my senior, yet she was livelier and much more spirted that I'd ever been. I'd never socialized with her outside the workplace, but was sure I'd enjoy her company. Learning to salsa was a lot more attractive than going home and being suffocated by Brandon's heavy brooding that was always thick in the air.

Now that Ava was back in his life, he was unreasonably giddy, but one wrong word from her or one missed call would send him on a downward spiral.

"I'll go," I agreed happily.

"Great! I guarantee you'll have a wonderful time," she assured me.

I doubted if I would have the "wonderful" time she predicted, but anything would be better than enduring Brandon's mood swings. I had no idea how I was going to singlehandedly get him committed, but tonight's salsa class would distract me from worrying about it.

Chapter 3

The Eyre Park Center, located in a neighboring town, was not the dreary place I'd envisioned. The center was bustling with people of all ages engaged in a variety of activities.

As I filled out the paperwork for the salsa class, both Veronica and the receptionist tried to persuade me to purchase an annual membership. That kind of commitment was out of the question, but after much prodding from Veronica, I agreed to a month's worth of salsa lessons.

The class was being held on an upper level, and on our way to the elevator, Veronica paused in front of the gymnasium and peered through the window. I stood next to her and observed women of various ages cycling in sync at a ridiculously fast speed. Buckets of sweat poured down their faces and drenched their workout wear.

"We could try that spin class the next time you visit," Veronica said with a deadpan expression.

"That's out of the question. I'd pass out trying to keep up with them. Whatever happened to normal cycling?"

"Folks get bored quick, so everything's constantly being updated. I can't keep up with all the newfangled exercise equipment, so I stick to dancing."

We progressed along the corridor and Veronica paused in front of a large room that featured a humongous rock-climbing wall. Three men were laughing and joking as they scaled the wall without wearing harnesses.

"They call that bouldering," Veronica informed.

"Wow, this place is much more upscale than I imagined," I mumbled, in awe and unable to tear my eyes away from the multiple sets of muscles that flexed and bulged as a group of men pulled themselves up the mountainous structure, competing with each other to get to the top. Though they were all beautifully masculine, one of the guys caught my attention. He was gorgeous with a thick head of prematurely silver hair. He stood out from the others with his uncanny good looks. Also, there seemed to be a magnetic force field that separated him from the rest of the pack.

"How'd you like to try climbing that forty-foot contraption?" Veronica asked. "Women and kids climb it, too. But the children have to wear harnesses."

I shook my head briskly. "No, thanks. I don't do well with heights."

At that moment the hot guy with the silvery hair did a daring feat that required swinging from one side of the wall to the other. He looked over his shoulder and smiled down at a cluster of people who stood below cheering him on. Judging from his unlined face, I assumed he was prematurely gray and probably somewhere in his early to mid-forties. As he dangled precariously, clutching a hook with one hand, he held my gaze and flicked a devilish grin at me.

Feeling my cheeks redden, I immediately dropped my gaze. A more outgoing person would have returned his smile, winked, or given him a thumbs-up for the astonishing feat he'd accomplished. But I was out of my depth. Too shy and self-conscious to attempt to even minimally interact with such a bold alpha male.

"We'd better get to our class," I said, turning away from the window.

"I believe that cute guy was making goo-goo eyes at you," Veronica teased as we moved toward the elevator.

Goo-goo eyes was the kind of antiquated terminology that she was fond of using.

"I hope the salsa instructor is patient with new students," I said, deliberately changing the subject. I was too unsettled by the unexpected flirtation from the brawny alpha to have a discussion about it with Veronica.

My track record for intimate relationships was nothing to be proud of. My last long-term involvement was with a married man—one of the therapists I'd taken Brandon to see. That relationship was probably unhealthier than my marriage and yet I'd remained available to him off and on for three years. I hadn't expected him to leave his wife for me, but seeing him on his terms only—during hasty lunchtime visits or whenever he could find an excuse to slip out of the house—did a job to my self-esteem. But I only had myself to blame. Eventually, I found the strength to put an end to the illicit affair.

There weren't any eligible bachelors in my age group living in Middletown, Pennsylvania and when I drove into the city for work, I seldom stuck around to go to Happy Hour or to attend any other nighttime activities where women and men tended to hook up. Being on the prowl for a man seemed so sad and futile, and quite frankly, I didn't have the emotional strength to throw my hat into the ring.

The last time anyone had flirted with me was at a horticulture convention about a year ago. His name was Clyde McCloskey and I became acquainted with him while he was giving a presentation titled "Insecticides for Landscapes." His discussion on the insecticides used to control landscape pests was so boring that attendees were falling asleep. At the conclusion, when he asked if there were any questions for him, no one uttered a sound. Being polite, I raised my hand and asked about soil drench versus foliar spray.

Clyde gave a long-winded response, causing people to start looking down at their watches and gathering their belongings. When participants began moving en masse toward the exit sign, Clyde asked if he and I could continue the discussion over drinks.

I didn't find him particularly attractive with his bushy mustache and thick-lensed eyeglasses, yet I surprised myself by agreeing to have a drink with him at the hotel bar. Despite the presence of a wedding band on his finger, we ended up in my hotel room, naked and in bed.

For the remaining days of the convention, we both ducked our heads down and scurried in opposite directions whenever we ran into each other. That was the last time I'd had sex, and I was beginning to feel lonely for male companionship. But I wasn't the least bit interested in a sexual entanglement with a dreamy-looking panty-melter who was probably a player with a long list of women on rotation.

A hot guy like the silver-haired rock climber would have me eating out of the palm of his hand, and I had enough common sense to know when to stay in my lane.

In class I surprised myself when I learned the basic On1 style rather quickly. Then the instructor moved on to more complicated left and right turns. After thirty minutes of concentrating on counting while dancing, I was relieved when she announced the class was over. Since the room was available to us for another ten minutes, she encouraged us to continue dancing—to be free with our movements and to improvise.

From her playlist she switched to a faster song, and I quickly moved to the back of the room where no one would notice me. The upbeat music with its rhythmic precision was both energizing and cathartic, allowing me to forget my troubles and lose myself in the driving force of the horns and drums. As I shook my shoulders, waved my arms, and twirled around, I ventured from the salsa to a weirdly wild mambo, or maybe I was doing the rumba. I had no idea.

In a zone, I briefly closed my eyes and envisioned myself vacationing on a tropical island holding a mojito in one hand and a margarita in the other.

My eyes popped open at the sound of the door opening and I was jolted by the sight of Mr. Silver-Haired Hotness entering the class.

Smiling, he craned his neck and scanned the room that was filled with women. His sparkly dark eyes landed on a tall, gorgeous brunette who appeared to be in her early twenties—maybe her late teens. He waved at her and she blushed and stopped dancing, seemingly embarrassed that she'd been caught freestyling.

It figured that a hot guy like him would be romantically involved with someone half his age. I felt a surge of resentment for the way he'd toyed with my emotions by tossing me that gleaming smile. Why had he bothered when he knew he was only interested in youthful arm candy?

No longer in the mood for dancing, I was ready to go home. Dealing with Brandon's hostility was preferable to being reminded that I was over the hill.

I tried to make eye contact with Veronica, but she was oblivious, swaying her hips in time to the music and giving no indication that she suffered from the acute hip pain she complained of at work.

The leggy brunette weaved through the throng of salsa dancers, making her way to the back of the room. I didn't want to hear a verbal exchange between the May-December lovers, and so I began inching my way forward, trying to get to Veronica.

But I wasn't quick enough. The young beauty's long strides with those coltish legs carried her to back of the room in record time.

"You promised not to come to my class. It's so humiliating, Dad," she complained, rolling her eyes and twirling her hair.

Dad! My mood instantly elevated as did my level of respect for Mr. Hotness.

"I thought the class ended ten minutes ago. I was only checking to make sure you hadn't gotten lost or anything," he explained in a teasing tone.

Clearly not feeling playful, the daughter rolled her eyes. "I have to grab my bag and my water bottle. Can you please wait for me in the car?" Behaving as if her father's concern for her well-being was a heinous crime, the girl stormed over to the cubbies where handbags and other personal items were stored during class.

I willed myself not to look in the hot guy's direction, but my neck swiveled around on its own accord. Our gazes met and I felt lightheaded.

He made an adorable face and then shrugged as if saying: *I'm a concerned parent; what's so terrible about that?* He was being playful, and but for a brief moment, I glimpsed a flicker of hurt in his eyes.

I commiserated by giving him a sad smile and shaking my head. I was painfully aware of the difficulties of parenthood.

He turned and left. To wait in the car, I supposed.

Meanwhile, I noticed that his daughter wasn't gathering her belongings. She and another young lady were standing near the cubbies taking selfies. Sharing the salsa class experience, they held up colorful pairs of maracas and posed with their mouths scrunched into those awful duck lips that I'd yet to understand the meaning of.

After the music ended, Veronica, apparently unwilling to call it a night, began mingling with the instructor and a few others from class. As I waited for her to wrap it up, I realized I was a bit parched. My sedentary body wasn't accustomed to so much physical activity and I could have kicked myself for forgetting to bring a bottle of water to class.

I cast a glance at Veronica, but she was still being a social butterfly. Not wanting to appear rude by rushing her, I left her alone and went out into the corridor in search of a water fountain. I didn't have to look very far. The fountain was on the opposite side of the corridor and so was Mr. Hotness! He was supposed to be in his car, but there he was, leaning against the fountain, and the shock of seeing him caused me to stop short and gawk at him. Like a deer caught in headlights.

"Hi, there. We meet again. Is it me, or is one of us stalking the other tonight?" He smiled playfully and the smile revealed crinkles at the corners of his eyes that added maturity and character to his otherwise youthful face.

Being serious by nature and not good at sardonic bantering, I couldn't think of one witty response. I possessed a warped sense of humor that hardly anyone got, so I refrained from cracking jokes with anyone other than Brandon—when he was in a rare good mood.

"My name's Jeff Schaeffer," he said, extending his hand.

"Claire Wilkins." I held out my hand and it was instantly swallowed inside his.

"My daughter, Allegra banished me to the car, and she's not gonna like that I'm still hanging around against her orders. But I decided to show her that teenagers aren't the only ones who get to be rebellious," he said with a wink.

Jeff didn't seem cocky at all. In fact, he had a boyish quality that was endearing. At the same time, he was incredibly masculine and exuded an aura of quiet power and control. Yet, despite his positive traits, every part of me wanted to turn around and run. Truth was I didn't want to give him an opportunity to reject me over my undeveloped conversational skills, and so I merely smiled and hoped he didn't think I was a mute idiot.

"I saw you outside the rock-climbing gym and thought I recognized you. Seeing you again in the salsa class made me realize that I don't know you..." His voice trailed off and he cleared his throat for effect. "But I'd like to. I don't see a wedding band," he said, looking down at my hand. "I don't have one, either." He held up his left hand

"I, um. I'm divorced," I sputtered.

"Yeah, me too. Two years. How long for you?"

"Sixteen."

Jeff whistled and furrowed his brow. "I'm still adjusting to being single, but I guess you've gotten the knack of it." He flashed another adorable smile and I noticed his even white teeth.

Jeff was a perfect male specimen. He was tall. Well over six feet with an olive complexion that was a stunning contrast against his silver hair. And his strong athletic body was muscular but not overly bulgy. As if he wasn't already good-looking enough, he also had long sweeping eyelashes that added to his sex appeal.

I felt frumpy in the shapeless sweats I'd chosen to wear to salsa class, but Jeff gazed at me admiringly. Like he thought I was hot! Slowly but surely, I began to get over my jitters and stopped stumbling over my words. I found myself inching closer to him and smiling a lot as my comfort level improved. As luck would have it, the moment I became relaxed, people began streaming out of class and filling the hallway.

Suddenly self-conscious, I took a few steps back. I wasn't quite sure if Jeff was flirting with me or merely being friendly, but I put a little distance between us. I also stood up straight, making sure that neither Veronica nor his daughter would misinterpret my body language and get the impression that we were up to anything.

"Hey, why don't we finish this conversation over lunch or dinner?" he boldly suggested, maintaining direct and steady eye contact. Then he pulled out his phone. "What's your number?" he asked in a rather assertive tone, looking down at the screen with his thumb poised to punch in the numbers.

Fully aware that an opportunity to go on a date with a sincerely nice guy who was also hot as hell wouldn't come around again anytime soon—if ever—I blurted out my number.

"Got it." He winked at me. "I'll call you in a couple of days to set something up."

"Sounds good." I raised my hand and fluttered my fingers in what I hoped looked like a sexy little wave, and then I slowly turned around.

I'd forgotten to quench my thirst, but that no longer mattered. In a euphoric haze, I felt like skipping back to salsa class, but realizing Jeff was watching me, I concentrated on moving as gracefully as possible and praying that I wouldn't stumble before I reached the door.

Inside, I let out a long breath and leaned against a wall to keep myself upright. A date! I was going out to lunch or dinner with the most incredibly gorgeous guy I'd ever met.

"You okay?" Veronica's voice brought me back to reality.

"Never been better."

"Well, you're looking off into space like you've gone bonkers. Did someone say something to upset you?" She looked around for the culprit, ready to defend me.

"No, everyone here seems really nice. I'm just a little lightheaded from all that dancing. But it was fun, Veronica," I quickly added. "Thanks for inviting me."

She took a moment to appraise me. "You're not going to drop the classes, are you?"

"Absolutely not," I said with a secret smile.

Chapter 4

I arrived home with Chinese takeout and was greeted by the scent of something cooking that was heavy on fried onions. Puzzled, I made my way to the kitchen and found Brandon standing at the stove with a spatula in his hand. To my chagrin, he'd gone against my wishes and Ava was in the kitchen with him. The tattooed harlot was perched atop the kitchen island sipping beer from a can while Brandon fussed over something that was sizzling and popping in the frying pan.

Being face-to-face with the person who'd caused my fragile son so much pain and angst caused my heartrate to speed up. Had it not been for the lingering elation over my upcoming date, I would have been frothing at the mouth. Seeing her sitting on a surface where we ate our meals made my blood boil. The sheer audacity! She had a wildness about her, and her numerous tattoos gave her an unclean appearance. Appraising her, I noticed that her black nail polish was badly chipped, adding to her unkempt look. I was seriously bothered by her slovenliness and wondered when she'd last washed the scuzzy-looking jeans she had on.

Brandon whirled around. "Hey, Mom. This is Ava...my girlfriend. I'm making cheeseburgers and jalapeño fries—her favorite," he gushed.

He was talking fast, obviously nervous. His eyes pleaded for me not to kick her out the house. To allow him this rare moment of happiness.

Expecting me to object to her presence in my home, Ava gave me a tight little defiant smile. As she waited for Brandon and me to begin bickering, her eyes flickered with excitement.

Refusing to give her the pleasure of seeing me unravel, I took a deep breath. "Hi, Ava. I've heard so much about you; it's nice to finally meet the young lady who has captured my son's heart." I nodded at the beer can. "I assume you're of legal drinking age." For Brandon's sake, I kept my tone cheerful, but my sneering smile informed Ava of my utter disdain for her.

"Yep, I'm legal." She gazed at me through mean eyes and then threw her head back and chugged down more beer. She cut an evil eye at me as she wiped her mouth with the back of her hand. That crude gesture forced me to look away. It was insane that my son had fallen for such an appalling girl.

Sensing the tension in the room, Brandon glanced at me. "You wanna try out my cooking, Mom?" The nervous way his Adam's apple bobbed up and down softened my heart.

I held up the bag of Chinese food. "No, thanks, I'll watch the news in my room and have dinner in bed. I'm sure you two lovebirds want to be alone." My words were followed by a significant look that warned him not to dare try and procreate with Ava in the sanctity of our home.

Brandon nodded in understanding, but I further enforced my rule by narrowing an eye at him. He scowled and nodded again. *I get it*, his surly expression said.

While Brandon and I communicated with our eyes, Ava set the beer can down and concentrated on picking at the remaining black polish from her thumbnail.

"You're letting the burgers burn," she said to Brandon in a reprimanding tone that pulled him back to her universe and out of mine. I was so irritated by her, I had to rush out of the kitchen.

What a bitch! I didn't know her full story, but she was clearly a damaged person. It was imperative that Brandon come to his senses and get her out of his life. What on Earth did he see in her? She was unattractive inside and out, and since it was clear by her attitude that she felt nothing but contempt for him, I wondered why she was deliberately trying to trap him with a pregnancy?

His father's money! Howard had a lucrative business and owned commercial real estate all over the state. But Ava was delusional if she thought Howard would part with any of his money for the offspring of the son he loathed.

On second thought, maybe she had latched onto Brandon so that she and her lesbian lover could have a baby. Using Brandon as a sperm donor was cheaper than paying for one. My foolish son didn't have a clue he was being used.

Suddenly panicked, I wondered if she was still ovulating. Sighing, I set the bag of Chinese food on the nightstand and decided I wasn't in the mood to worry over Brandon tonight. I'd had a wonderful chance encounter with someone who wanted to get to know me better and I preferred to daydream about my upcoming date than agonize over the possibility of Brandon impregnating his so-called girlfriend.

I'd have a stern talk with him after work tomorrow. If he was grown enough to even consider the lunacy of bringing a child into the world, then it was time for him to become self-reliant.

Veronica was right; implementing tough love was the only way to prevent Brandon from ruining his life.

First thing in the morning, I trekked down the hall to peek in on Brandon and was grateful to find him sleeping alone.

As usual his TV was on with the Xbox hooked up to it. A video game was frozen on the screen. I moved deeper inside his room to turn off the TV and had to navigate around Xbox discs and their cases, among a variety of objects that were carelessly strewn about.

Glancing at Brandon as he snored softly, I noticed that a set of controllers were entwined in the bedding. Not the usual solitary controller and the headset he used to communicate with online players. The two separate controllers indicated he'd been playing with a partner.

Empty beer cans were scattered about, and since Brandon didn't drink alcohol (he hated the taste), I concluded that he'd disobeyed my rules and had invited Ava to his bedroom at some point last night while I was asleep.

His comic book collection, the only possessions that were important enough to be kept organized inside sneaker boxes, was spilled onto the floor on the opposite side of where Brandon slept, confirming my suspicions that his girlfriend had been in his room.

Apparently Ava hadn't minded the squalid conditions. In fact, she'd added to the chaos with the beer cans and piles of comic books.

Livid, I was on the verge of shaking Brandon awake to chastise him for breaking the house rules, but the distant ding of the microwave sent me hurrying out of his room and down the stairs.

In the kitchen, which still stank of onions, I found Ava stirring almond milk into a bowl of instant oatmeal she'd helped herself to. Greasy, unwashed pots and pans were on top of the stove and dirty dishes filled the sink. She and Brandon were both disgusting pigs!

"Why're you still here?" Clutching my robe, I gaped at Ava like she was an evil apparition.

She shrugged. "I had a little too much to drink and Brandon didn't want me driving. It's no big deal."

"It's a big deal to me. This is my home, and if memory serves, I didn't give my son permission to have an overnight guest."

"Are you saying I should have risked getting a DUI? Or possibly killing myself or others?"

"You could have called an Uber," I replied, shaking my head. Brandon couldn't have chosen a more unpleasant girl. "Listen, Ava, Brandon told me about your plan to conceive a child with him. He can barely take care of himself, so why would you want to make him a father before he's ready?"

"I'm ready," she said, giving me a challenging look.

"Do you even have a job?"

"No, but I'll get state benefits to help out."

I sighed. "Do you realize how ridiculous you sound?"

"No more ridiculous than you getting pregnant so that Brandon's dad would be forced to marry you and be saddled with paying for your education."

"That's a lie," I spat.

"Well, that's what your son told me," she said with a smug look on her face.

I had no idea where Brandon had gotten the idea that I'd trapped his father into marrying me. I didn't get pregnant with him until well over a year after our wedding, and Howard and I both were ecstatic over the birth of our son. But Howard's interest had waned after he began building his real estate business and he went from being a caring and concerned parent to one who treated his son like he was nothing more than an irritating distraction.

Perhaps Brandon had decided that his conception had been unplanned or a ploy to trap his father due to Howard's indifference toward him when he was a young boy. Disinterest turned to disdain when Brandon became a teen. I was certain that the way Howard doted on his new children while ignoring Brandon played a huge part in our son's self-esteem issues.

I swallowed back a lump of sorrow as I recalled Howard coming home from work with his phone pressed to his ear, still conducting business.

As a toddler, Brandon would greet his father excitedly. He'd run to Howard and wrap his chubby little arms around his legs. Aggravated,

Howard would extricate himself from Brandon's grasp while frowning and gesturing for me to control the boy.

"Why does he always have to be so clingy?" Howard had said in a harsh whisper as I struggled to contain Brandon who was trying to wriggle out of my arms.

Without so much as a pat on his son's head, Howard would head for his study and close the door, and I would be left to pacify Brandon as he cried for his uncaring daddy.

Looking back, Brandon was around two years old when he went from a happy child to one with stormy moods. At the time, I had attributed his behavior to his age, buying into the myth about the terrible twos.

But I now realized that Brandon was only two years old when his father had first begun to rebuff him.

Subconsciously, I'd been overcompensating for Howard's rejection of our son ever since. There was no question that Brandon and I both needed therapy. And once and for all, I was going to insist that we seek treatment together.

I sighed heavily as I glanced at Ava who was digging into the bowl of oatmeal. Her unwelcome presence in my kitchen, which was an awful mess and smelled of last night's onions and burned burgers, was simply too much for this hour of the morning. I was in desperate need of a jolt of caffeine, and could feel a headache threatening to spring from the base of my skull.

"I have to go upstairs and get ready for work," I said wearily as I rubbed the back of my neck. "I'd appreciate it if you'd gather your things and leave before I come back down for my morning coffee."

"Cool. Not a problem." Dismissing me, she stared down at her phone, using the thumb with the badly chipped black polish to rapidly swipe the screen.

Chapter 5

When I heard the muted sound of my cell phone, which was tucked inside a desk drawer at the bottom of my purse, I ignored it. My department expenditures had exceeded the money allocated in the quarterly budget and I was busy crunching numbers, trying to figure out where to cut corners. It was frustrating work, making me sweaty and anxious. Dealing with the departmental budget was as tedious and grueling as preparing my taxes.

Since work-related calls came through the telephone console on my desk, I figured it was Brandon ringing my cell. Always the harbinger of bad news, he only called when catastrophic events occurred at home: the HVAC system had broken down; an outdoor pipe had clogged and sewage had backed up in the garage causing an unbearable stench inside the house; a tree had fallen during a storm, breaking a window and blocking the driveway.

Whenever there was a household emergency, Brandon, who wasn't handy at all, simply picked up the phone and dumped the bad news on me and waited grumpily while I resolved the situation that was interfering with his enjoyment of life.

I, on the other hand, would have to interrupt my day and take the time and effort to track down an affordable professional to do the job, schedule an appointment, and then in many cases, max out a credit card to pay the bill.

The phone stopped ringing briefly and then began again. I eyed my watch. It was only ten in the morning, and Brandon seldom got up before noon. Fearing that a terrible catastrophe had occurred at home, I yanked the desk drawer open and groped through my purse until my hand landed on the oblong shape of my phone.

I looked at the screen and didn't recognize the number, which upset me even more. Had something terrible happened to Brandon? Was this the call that every mother dreaded?

"Hello?" I said in a shaky, fearful voice.

"Claire?"

The voice on the other end of the phone reverberated through my system like a series of thunder claps. It wasn't some stranger at a hospital or a police station with devastating news that would destroy me...it was *him!*

"Jeff, how are you?" I tried to sound as normal as possible as I slowly recovered from the shock of hearing his voice. He said he'd call in a few days, not the very next morning, and I was taken completely off guard.

"Did I catch you at a bad time?"

I glanced at the worrisome expense reports that were scattered on my desk. "No, not at all."

"I was wondering if you were free for lunch."

"Lunch? Uh..."

Oh, God. The outfit I'd thrown together this morning screamed soccer mom. After my run-in with Ava, I'd been so frazzled, I snatched from the closet the first pair of slacks and top that my hands touched. I had on cotton slacks that were too loose in the butt area and a scoop neck top with bees and flowers embroidered on the front. The gimmicky top was okay for work but inappropriate for a lunch date with a hot guy.

I studied my reflection in the glass desk cover and recoiled. My hair looked drab and lifeless and needed a trim, my skin was blotchy, and my eyebrows were badly in need of waxing.

"Would you rather make it dinner?" he asked after my lengthy hesitation.

"Yes, dinner sounds great."

"Do you like Italian?"

"Love it." I was sure he wasn't referring to pizza or stromboli, which had been the extent of my Italian-eating experience for the past ten years or more. However, the distant memory of handmade pasta, intriguing sauces, and fresh bread dipped in olive oil made my mouth water.

"Good, I'll make reservations at Vincenzo's—in the city. Have you eaten there?"

"No, I haven't."

"You'll love it. I was there with a client a few weeks ago and the scaloppini of veal was incredible. What's your address? I'll pick you up at seven."

"Text me the time of the reservation and I'll meet you there," I replied quickly after picturing Brandon and possibly Ava lurking around, being rude and antisocial when Jeff arrived. Additionally, it was too embarrassing to even try to explain the big hole in the dining room wall, the result of one of Brandon's explosive episodes.

"All right. I'll text the information. I look forward to seeing you again, Claire," he said before hanging up.

"I look forward to seeing you, too." Ugh, I hated the way my voice came out sounding so mushy and dumb, and so I quickly hung up.

I sat at my desk and cringed for a full five minutes. Why couldn't

I have responded with something flirtatious or witty? Sadly, I wasn't wired that way.

"I moved to Middletown eight months ago," Jeff said as the waiter poured the wine.

"Where're you from originally?"

"Los Angeles."

I raised my brows. "You left glamourous L.A. to come to our little boring town?"

"Business brought me here. But Middletown's not boring to me. I find it charming and refreshing after the pretentiousness of Los Angeles." He swirled the wine in the glass and sniffed it several times before tasting it. Then he laughed suddenly. "Okay, I know that looked like a total jerk move, typical of a pompous ass from L.A., but I can explain."

"I'm all ears." Thoroughly charmed, I leaned in a little. I loved his eyes. They were medium brown with flecks of gold that sparkled whenever he smiled.

"Well, my ex-wife was a sommelier."

"A what?"

"Someone with extensive knowledge of wine and food pairings. She taught me a little about wine and it's a habit now to swirl and sniff," he said, laughing.

When he spoke of his ex, I instantly envisioned a beautiful, sophisticated woman with exquisite taste. Although I'd taken the time to curl my hair, had gotten a mani-pedi during my lunch break, and was wearing a sexy, form-fitting lace dress with a plunging V-neckline, I still was no raving beauty. Jeff's eyes had lit up when I entered the restaurant and he told me I looked beautiful, but I wondered if I looked like a hick compared to his ex-wife. If his tanned, gorgeous daughter was any indication of how the women in his life looked, then I couldn't begin to compete.

His eyes turned serious. "It was weird, but when I first noticed you watching me while I was climbing, there was this flash of recognition. You seemed so familiar." He tilted his head. "I mentioned that already, didn't I?"

I nodded. "Yes, when we were talking in the hall outside my salsa class."

"Right," he responded, eyes narrowed in recollection. "Wanna know a secret?"

"Sure."

"I didn't come into your class to check on Allegra. I wanted to get a closer look at you."

My heart quickened and I went total schoolgirl, fidgeting with my hair, blushing, and smiling. "How'd you know where to find me?"

"I don't want to freak you out and make you think I'm a stalker, but when you walked away from the climbing gym, I climbed midway down and jumped the rest of the way. I wanted to catch up with you and ask where we'd met before. But I wasn't fast enough. I saw you get on the elevator and noticed that it went down to the lower level. The only classes being held downstairs were salsa and mixed martial arts. I don't mean to sound sexist, but I didn't picture you throwing punches, doing a spinning back kick, or engaging in a double leg takedown and pinning your opponent down in submission as you choked him out with your legs."

I made a face. "That sounds horrible."

"My point, exactly. It's a violent sport and I figured a demure lady like you would prefer dancing to fighting." He chuckled and I laughed along with him.

It was obvious that Jeff had a great sense of humor. The evening had just begun, and I'd already smiled more in a half hour than I'd had in the past few months.

Our food arrived and we both marveled over the beautiful presentation before digging in.

"Do you have kids?" he asked.

"A son. Brandon. He's twenty."

"Is Brandon in college?"

I felt myself stiffen. "No, he decided to take a semester off. To sort of figure things out." I shrugged and squirmed uncomfortably.

"College isn't for everyone. It's sad the way so many kids can't find jobs after graduating. They're left saddled with huge student loans that they can't afford to repay. It wasn't like that back when I went to school. If you went to college, you were guaranteed some kind of employment, but it's not like that anymore."

My shoulders relaxed. I appreciated that Jeff didn't automatically start suggesting ways for me to whip Brandon into shape.

"Your daughter seems like she has it together. Is she in college?"

"No, Allegra's only sixteen. She's still in high school."

"Oh, I thought she was older."

"Yeah, she looks older with all the makeup and the bossy attitude, but she's still a baby. She lives in L.A. with her mom and I had to bribe her to get her to spend the summer with me. I promised her a car, but we're not in agreement over the make and model. I want her behind the wheel of something sturdy and safe and she wants a sports car."

He held out his hands in exasperation, but there was pride in his eyes. Irrationally, I felt a twinge of envy, wondering what it felt like to parent a child whose only flaw was being bossy and desiring a sports car.

For a long moment, Jeff regarded me with such an admiring smile I became embarrassed and uncomfortable.

"What?" I finally asked.

"You're so pretty. You have an understated beauty that sneaks up on you and then, bam! It knocks you off your feet."

"I don't know about that." I giggled nervously and fussed with my hair.

"Wanna know the first thing I noticed about you?" he asked.

"No idea." My heart started picking up speed again.

"Your smile."

I furrowed my brows.

"Yeah, while we were climbing and you were watching through the window, you had a faint smile. It looked mysterious, like Mona Lisa, and I wondered what you were thinking. Maybe that's why I thought I recognized you. You reminded me of a magnificent work of art."

At this point I was grinning like an idiot, eating up all the praise he was lavishing on me. Unable to take any more, I held up my hands. "Listen, I am definitely out of your league. You're way too smooth for me, Jeff."

"No, you've got me wrong. I'm not a smooth talker with great lines. Every word I've spoken is the honest truth." He smiled briefly and then he turned serious, meeting my eyes in a meaningful way, and then holding my gaze. "When we were out in the hallway talking, I felt an instant connection with you, and there was no way I was going to let you get away again. Not without getting your number."

He looked even more handsome when he wore a serious expression.

"So, what kind of business pulled you away from sunny L.A.?" I asked, trying to take the focus off me so I could pull myself together and catch my breath. I looked down and moved food around my plate. Being with Jeff had me too excited to actually eat.

Jeff chewed his food and swallowed before answering. "I'm a private consultant. I help companies that are bleeding cash find out where the bullets are coming from so they can start patching up the wounds."

I gazed at him quizzically.

He smiled indulgently. "Okay, say a company is experiencing financial losses, but can't figure out why. Business is good and money is coming in, yet they're still in the red. They call me in to take a much closer look—to really scrutinize their spending habits, and I always find out where the money is going."

"What're some of your findings?"

"Courtside season tickets to Laker games for the entire management team. A vice president with a penthouse apartment in New York for weekend getaways with his paramour. Company cars for lower management—not your typical Fords and Chevies or Toyotas, but expensive Benzes and BMWs. The assistants of senior staff members have their own full-time assistants."

"You're kidding."

"I kid you not. Oh, it gets worse. I won't name the business, but a certain Fortune 500 company paid for five-hundred-dollars-an-hour escorts to entertain clients whenever they came to town." Jeff laughed heartily and he looked so boyishly cute at the moment, I could have grabbed his face and kissed him until we were both breathless.

The effect Jeff was having on me was slightly scary. He was awakening feelings and sensations that I'd believed were long dead.

He was quite the conversationalist—a very interesting person, but after a while, his voice became a distant hum. I could see his full, luscious lips moving, but it felt like everything was going in slow motion. Shockingly, I found myself wondering how his ripped body looked naked. Was he was packing anything of substance, and if so, was he good in bed? Oh, my God, it was shameful, but I had so much pent-up sexual tension, I would have willingly spread my legs for him right there on top of the table.

Well, maybe not on top of the table, but it wouldn't have taken much prodding to get me in the restroom for a frantic quickie.

Jeff had no idea that I wanted to tell him to shut up and fuck me! Shocked by my own slutty thoughts, I could feel my face redden.

"Are you okay?" Jeff asked, giving me an odd look.

"I'm fine," I said, smiling demurely.

Outside the restaurant, as we waited for the valet to bring our cars, an evening breeze fluttered past us. "Cold?" Jeff asked, putting an arm around me without waiting for my reply.

In that moment, I could have easily purred like a contented cat. My life had been so shitty, so sad and hopeless, I had long ago given up on the notion of romantic love. But when Jeff lowered his head and kissed me, I became audacious enough to believe that there was a glimmer of hope that happiness could exist for me.

Chapter 6

I stood in the doorway of Brandon's bedroom with my arms crossed. I'd already said his name twice, but he hadn't responded. He sat on the edge of his bed, holding a controller, engrossed in the avatars on the screen that moved around an imaginary football field. I couldn't tell if he was unaware of my presence or simply ignoring me.

Wearing a headset, he bellowed into the microphone: "Get 'em! Whoa, good hit, Newsflash202! Move it, move it, man. Yeah. Good job!"

In the next moment, he jumped to his feet and pumped his fist. "Touchdown," he yelled in triumph and then talked trash to the players he was competing with.

It baffled me that someone who'd never played football a day in his life and had no interest in any athletics was such a skilled player when he was simulating a sport with a controller in his hand.

Being a social outcast and not having any real-life friends, Brandon's smiles and laughter during interactions with his Xbox buddies usually gave me a modicum of comfort. He was always so angry and such a recluse, it was reassuring to see him making connections, even if it was only with anonymous people whom he only knew by screen names like Newsflash202.

But tonight I wasn't moved by his happiness and contentment. I was furious that he'd blatantly disobeyed my request to clean up the mess that he and that dreadful girl had made in the kitchen.

Although he'd turned into a slob the moment he'd reached puberty, I'd always been adamant that his slovenly ways had to be confined to his own bedroom and he usually complied with my wishes. It boggled my mind why he was being so defiant. He'd had all day while I was at work and the entire evening while I was at dinner with Jeff to clean up the kitchen. Now it was after eleven o'clock, and he not only hadn't bothered to clean up the mess from last night, but he'd added to the chaos. And so had Ava.

On the island was a puddle of red juice, globs of grape jelly, slices of bread spilling from a gaping loaf of bread, and an uncapped jar of peanut butter was left on the countertop with a butter knife protruding from it. And the remnants of Ava's breakfast had been left on the kitchen table as well.

"Brandon!" The aggravation of having to call his name for the third time caused my voice to climb to a screechy pitch. When he continued to ignore me, I marched over to the surge protector on the floor and used the tip of my shoe to click the red button, shutting off the TV, the computer, his phone charger, and whatever else was plugged into the numerous outlets.

In a state of disbelief, Brandon's eyes bounced back and forth from the darkened TV screen to my face. "I was in the middle of a game. Why'd you fuckin' do that?"

"Don't use that language with me."

"Well, don't come in my room acting like a whack job," he spat, his face contorted in anger. He looked furious enough to strike me, and although I knew he wouldn't dare get physical with me, my body tensed in expectation of the loud boom that would occur when he punched or kicked a wall or sent a large inanimate object crashing to the floor.

Surprisingly, he didn't do anything except quietly seethe for a few moments. With his fists balled, he breathed in and out rapidly, his chest heaving up and down. When he moved toward the power strip and bent down to power up all the devices I'd shut down, I blocked his path. He sighed and gave a little laugh of disbelief, like I was the most irrational person he'd ever encountered.

"I've repeatedly told you that I'm not your maid, Brandon."

He shuffled from foot-to-foot. "I said I'm gonna clean the damn kitchen before I go to bed, so get off my back!"

"No, I'm not going to get off your back," I said stubbornly. "I told you to clean up behind yourself last night and I reminded you again when I came home from work. Now, here it is after eleven at night and you've not only refused to do what I asked of you, but you added to the chaos with spilled juice and peanut butter and jelly. And your slob of a girlfriend didn't even have the common decency to wash the breakfast dishes she left behind."

"Is that what this is about—Ava? She's not perfect, but she's not a bad person, either. I don't know why you hate her so much."

I started to deny hating her, but it was pointless to lie. "This is not about Ava. It's about you totally defying my wishes. What am I missing? Why do you think it's unreasonable to expect you to clean up after you've prepared food?"

"Maybe I wouldn't have had to resort to making fucking peanut and jelly for dinner if you'd brought home dinner like you're supposed to."

"Supposed to?" I repeated in disbelief. "You're going to be twenty-one on your next birthday. By law, my obligation to provide for you ended when you turned eighteen. But I continue to try and make life easy for you out of love."

"That's a crock of shit. Whatever it is you *think* you do for me, you do out of guilt."

I blinked. "What?"

"You let Dad treat me like shit and your guilt is eating you alive."

"I did no such thing. After he started his business, your father became aloof and he detached himself from both of us, Brandon. The only way I knew how to protect you from a man who wasn't present in your life was to divorce him."

"Wow, great strategizing, Mom. I applaud your parenting skills," he said sarcastically.

I shot him a confused look.

"Divorcing Dad only drove him further away. Do you know what life has been like for me, having a father that acts like he barely knows me?"

"And you think it's my fault?"

"Yeah," he said, poking out his lips.

"If you believe I'm responsible for your father's unwillingness to be involved in your life, then you seriously need therapy to work through your misplaced anger and blame issues. I'm willing to join you if that'll help."

"I already told you a million times that therapy is bullshit and I'm not going. Fuck that!" Brandon's foul language was getting to me, but I had bigger issues to contend with.

"Therapy is no longer up for debate. You have to see someone if you expect to continue living under my roof. In the meantime, I insist that you go downstairs and get to work in the kitchen. It looks and smells like a pigsty." I scrunched my face, emphasizing my disgust.

"Did I hear you right? Did you say I have to fucking leave if I don't see a fucking shrink?" He took menacing steps toward me.

I pressed a palm against his chest. "You're behaving in a threatening manner, Brandon, and I don't like it."

"How am I behaving threateningly?" He held up his long lean arms that were sinewy with small muscles, a gift of youth and not from putting in any strenuous effort.

"You're getting in my face. Look, clearly something has to give. You can't go on like this...loafing around, playing video games, and feeling sorry for yourself. You obviously need help to get motivated about life."

"I *am* motivated. I'm planning a family with Ava, and I guarantee you I'll be a better father than that piece-of-shit sperm donor of mine."

"But you can't provide for a child," I rationalized. "Do you think it's a good idea to deliberately bring a child into the world when you're not even making plans to earn an income?"

"Ava's got it all worked out. She'll get state assistance for a little while and then she's going to fake like the kid has asthma or something and then she'll get social security benefits. She knows all the ins and outs of beating the system."

I let out a mournful groan and rubbed my temple. Listening to Brandon's ridiculous plan to leach off the government was painful. It was late and I couldn't deal with his irrational thinking for another second.

"I'm tired, Brandon, and I'm going to bed. We'll talk about your absurd plan for fatherhood when I get home from work tomorrow."

"There's nothing to talk about. It's my life and you can't dictate how I live it."

"What about Ava's girlfriend? How does she fit into the equation?"

"Ava said being with Muffy was just a phase."

"So, why're they still living together?"

"I don't know, Mom. Ava's trying to let her down gently, I guess." He shrugged and I could tell that he had no idea what Ava planned on doing about her other lover.

I shook my head and sighed. "You need to rethink your plans with Ava, but in the meantime, please do what I asked you to do. The kitchen is filthy and it's reeking."

"Okaaaay! How many times do I have to say I'll take care of it before I go to bed?" He moved around me and clicked the switch of the surge protector. A hum filled the room as a myriad of electronic equipment whirred back to life.

He rolled onto his bed and picked up the Xbox controller.

"Brandon, put down that controller and do what I asked...now," I said adamantly.

"Do it now or what?" He cast a challenging glance at me and his eyes were filled with what looked like a mixture of hatred and simmering rage.

But why was he so infuriated with *me*—the only person in the world who had loved him unconditionally and had done everything in my power to give him a good life?

He was an ungrateful overgrown child and I only had myself to blame. I'd given too much and expected too little from him, but the level of disrespect that he was exhibiting tonight was intolerable.

"Forget about the kitchen; I'll clean it myself. But when I get home from work tomorrow, I expect you to have packed your things and moved out." I couldn't believe those words had come out of my mouth, but I forged on. "Making it on your own will give you the reality check you need to see how easy you've had it. I don't want you calling and asking me for any money because I'm not going to give you a dime if you don't try to help yourself. If you get a job and need money for work essentials or carfare, I'll help you out. What I really want is for you to enroll in school. It doesn't have to be college, per se. It would be perfectly fine for you to go to a trade school or anywhere that teaches practical skills."

"You asked me to leave, but you're still trying to control my life."

"I'm trying to help guide you in the right direction."

"I don't need your guidance." He looked at me and shrugged nonchalantly. "I'll be out of here tomorrow."

"Good." I left his room and went to my room and changed from the lace dress to a pair of sweats and tank top, and then I went downstairs to tackle the kitchen. I scrubbed pots and pans, wiped off countertops and cabinets, swept and mopped the floor and then took out the smelly trash.

It took over an hour to complete the job. After taking a shower, it was past midnight when I finally crawled into bed. I was exhausted and exhilarated at the same time. Finding the strength to finally give Brandon an ultimatum was liberating, but it was also a little embarrassing that it had taken me so long to put my foot down.

Tough love and therapy were exactly what he needed. Brandon would thank me when he became an emotionally healthy and self-sufficient adult.

Chapter 7

W hen I entered the wrought-iron gates at work, I noticed a throng of people bedecked with green-and-white volunteer buttons standing in the courtyard. Shannon Teal, the head of the volunteer department, was giving them her spiel about how important they were to the success of the zoo. I tried to slip past the group undetected, but Shannon caught me and waved me over.

Resignedly, I plodded toward them with my coffee thermos in hand. After the long and eventful night I'd had—the dreamy date with Jeff followed by the confrontation with Brandon and then late-night kitchen-cleaning—the last thing I felt like doing was engaging with a pack of strangers before I'd had my second cup of coffee of the morning.

But duty called. It was my plan to introduce myself and say something short and sweet about the work my department did and then scamper off to the horticulture building to unwind and get my bearings before taking on a brand-new work day.

Unfortunately, Shannon had other plans for me.

"This is Walter Caulfield and he has quite the green thumb." She nodded at an older gentleman who was tall and broad-shouldered with salt-and-pepper hair, and gleaming hazel eyes. He wasn't bad-looking for his age.

Walter wasn't shy at all. He chimed right in after Shannon introduced him. "I took up gardening after I retired, and man-oh-man, I have to say that I missed my calling. I wasted thirty good years working as an engineer. I'd probably have fewer gray hairs had I worked with plants at the beginning of my career. But it's never too late. I'm eager to get started," he said, smiling and rubbing his hands together.

Both Walter and Shannon gazed at me as if expecting me to reply with a witty response, but I'd never been known as a jokester, and even if I were, it was too early in the morning for clever banter. All I could manage was to give them both a weak smile.

Shannon quickly filled the tense silence. "I'll bring Walter over as soon as we finish up orientation."

"Great," I muttered.

Walter winked at me and I couldn't decide if he was a dirty old man or the friendly grandfatherly type. I offered him an uncertain, twitchy smile before taking off.

Sitting at my desk in the office, I was staring off into space thinking about Brandon and second-guessing my decision to put him out when my staff began trickling in.

"You okay?" asked Meghan, a twenty-something, cute and bubbly young woman who was the most recent hire in the department. Meghan was such a sweetheart, she never balked or complained when Veronica behaved as if she were her supervisor, designating tasks for her to do. Ironically, Meghan had a higher position and earned more money than Veronica, and it was only a matter of time before Meghan pulled rank and rebelled against bossy Veronica. I'd seen it happen with every new hire. They were initially intimidated by Veronica's vast knowledge and experience, but that always changed after they realized that Veronica was the low man on the totem pole in our department.

"I'm fine," I said to Meghan.

"Anything you want me to do before I head over to the carnivorous plant display?"

I thought about Winking Walter. "As a matter of fact, there is. Would you stop by Volunteer Services? Shannon Teal has assigned a volunteer to our department. He has a lot of horticulture experience and I'm sure he'll be a great addition to our staff. I'd appreciate if you'd show him the ropes and let him shadow you today."

Meghan's sunny expression darkened a little. No one enjoyed being shadowed by a volunteer. Having to interrupt a busy workday to show someone the ropes was beyond inconvenient; it was sheer torture. But I had a lot on my mind. Personal matters to work through and perhaps a tension-filled phone conversation with Brandon that I didn't want anyone eavesdropping on.

After all seven staff members had checked in and then gone off to their various work stations around the zoo, I tried to focus on the damned quarterly report that I'd failed to make any progress on yesterday. But I couldn't concentrate.

My mind kept flitting back to dinner with Jeff, prompting me to break into a dreamy smile, but the moment I felt an inkling of happiness, I'd think about Brandon and all my joy would evaporate.

Would my son become a homeless person? As far as I knew, there weren't any homeless shelters in Middletown. So, what would Brandon do? Where would he go? I imagined him making his way to the city living under a bridge inside a tent or a cardboard box.

Other than crashing at Ava's place with her and her lesbian lover, where else would he go? And since she'd mistreated him so badly the last time he'd impulsively moved in with her, this time would probably be far worse with him trying to share her with a disgruntled girlfriend.

Oh, God, it was all so disgusting and sordid. The most secure person in the world wouldn't be able to survive such a horribly dysfunctional arrangement, and Brandon was much too high-strung and emotionally unstable to become a part of the twisted triangle that Ava had lured him into.

Feeling panicked and experiencing a complete change of heart, I called Brandon's cell. When he didn't pick up, I sent a lengthy text urging him to stay put. I told him we'd both been angry and a bit irrational last night. I said that we needed to revisit the subject of his living arrangements with level heads.

I hit "send" and waited to hear from him. After fifteen minutes had dragged by without a call or a text, I dove into my work. It was best to stay busy. Had I kept my focus on Brandon, I would have left work early and raced home to check on him.

My phone pinged with a text message around noon. I anxiously grabbed my phone and looked down at the message on the screen.

Had a great time last night. Hope we can get together again. If you're free Saturday, I'd love to take you sailing. A day trip to Cape May.

I scowled at the message, feeling annoyance instead of joy. Ordinarily, I would have been extremely flattered that Jeff wanted to see me again. I'd never gone sailing before and it seemed really romantic. Unfortunately, my anxiety over Brandon was so profound, I couldn't be bothered to take the time to respond to the message.

I called Brandon once more. Left another message and waited. When twenty minutes passed, I grabbed my handbag and rushed toward the door. Outside, my quick getaway was interrupted. Winking Walter and Meghan were striding toward the horticulture building, and I groaned inwardly. They were the last two people I wanted to see.

Meghan, who was usually cheerful, looked frazzled and worn down. But Walter's eyes were alit with excitement as if he'd been feeding off Meghan's abundant energy.

"Welp, I've seen it all today," Walter said, grinning and rolling his eyes heavenward. "Never before have I seen a Venus flytrap or any of those other carnivorous plants in action. Only on TV and in the movies. Seeing a plant eating bugs and whatnot in person was a heck of an experience. This little lady, Meghan, had me feeding those blasted things like they were pets. And if that wasn't bad enough, she had me massaging their outside surfaces to get 'em to digest the insects." Walter was talking a mile a minute. He sucked in air, prepared to continue, but I used that opportunity to interrupt him.

"Can't talk right now, Walter. I have an emergency," I said in a breathless rush of words.

"Are you leaving for the day?" Meghan asked, sounding panicked.

"Yes, I have a situation at home. Family emergency."

"Well, what should I do with Walter? I have that meeting with the summer planning committee in ten minutes, remember?" Her widened eyes implored me to get her off the hook with Walter.

I was about to tell Meghan to let him accompany her to the staff meeting, but it was evident that she was desperate to get rid of him. He'd probably been talking her ears off for hours, and she needed a break.

"Why don't you walk Walter over to the greenhouse and introduce him to Veronica? I'm sure she could use some help." Veronica was pretty chatty herself. Maybe she and Walter would hit it off.

"The greenhouse, yay!" Walter winked and made a double-clicking sound in his mouth. Then he engaged in his version of a happy dance, and I noticed he was rather light on his feet. A spry older man who probably had a way with the ladies.

I couldn't tell if he was sincerely delighted about being shuffled off to the greenhouse or if he was being sarcastic. In addition to his talkativeness and all that unnecessary winking, there was something else about Walter that made me uneasy. Something was off about him, but I couldn't put my finger on it. I made a mental note to tell Shannon that I didn't think he was a good fit for my department.

There were none of the usual sounds. No TV blaring. No computer-ized gunshots from a video game, and I could tell Brandon wasn't home before I'd gone upstairs and checked his room.

I stood in the doorway of his bedroom, taking in the quiet, the emptiness. He'd cleared out everything except his desk and a swivel chair. His house key was left on top of the desk, and the sight of it put a lump in my throat. Although he'd moved in with Ava before, this time was different. This time I'd kicked him out, and I feared that I'd unwittingly put something awful into motion—changing the course of his life in an unalterable way.

The sensation of impending doom was so overwhelming, I clamped a hand over my mouth and tried not to cry. Despite my best efforts, tears welled in my eyes and soon ran down my face.

Brandon was so broken...so fragmented, he was ill-equipped to make it on his own. I should have simply made peace with the fact that I'd have to take care of him for the rest of my life instead of tossing him to the wolves. And Ava was definitely a wolf. There was no telling what type of unlawful and immoral behavior she'd lure him into.

I could hear the muffled sound of my phone ringing from inside my handbag that was looped over my shoulder. I dug out my phone and could have screamed with joy when I saw Brandon's name on the screen.

"Brandon, where are you? Are you all right?"

"I'm great, Mom. I'm at Ava's."

"Do you want me to come and get you? What's her address? I can come right now."

"No, I'm settling in. It's all good."

"What about the uh, other girl, Muffin?"

"Muffy," he corrected. "She's cool. Everything's cool."

"Listen, sweetheart, I was wrong to force you into such an unhealthy environment—such an insane living situation. You don't have to be there, Brandon. You can come home. "

"I know, I read your texts. But see, Mom, I don't view living with Ava and Muffy as insane."

I hated Muffy's name and in my mind, I saw her as the stereotypical Butch-type, a boxy-shaped woman who dressed in men's clothes and shaved the hair on one side of her head.

"People should be free to love whoever they want," he continued. "Can you tell me where it's written that you're only allowed to love one person?"

I gnawed on my bottom lip as I listened to Brandon spew what sounded like Ava's warped outlook on life and love. "But you don't love more than one person do you, Brandon? You don't have romantic feeling for this Muffy person, do you? You only love Ava. And I assume Muffy loves Ava and not you."

"We're cool. I love Muffy, you know, like a friend."

"But who's the one benefiting from this new philosophy of yours? Sounds to me that Ava's the only one that's going to have her cake and eat it too."

"You don't understand, Mom. We're all trying to make this work for the sake of the baby."

"Is she pregnant?" I screeched hysterically.

"Not yet, but we're working on it."

"Oh, Brandon. Sweetie. You need to rethink this before it's too late," I said in a cajoling tone.

"My mind is made up, and if you can't respect my decision, then just leave me alone."

"Okay, Brandon. But...but—"

"It's all good," he insisted. "Muffy found a job at a plant in Secane. They make carburetors, and she says they're hiring. Ava's going to put together a resume for me."

I couldn't begin to imagine what he'd say about his previous work experience. "What about Ava? Is she going to apply for a job at the plant, too, or is she going to relax at home while her two devoted lovers toil on her behalf?"

"You don't have to get sarcastic. I'm hanging up."

"Wait...I was only asking. Also, I'm curious to know if you do conceive a child, will this Muffy person have a role in its life?"

Brandon let out a groan, as if my question was idiotic. "Yeah, she's going to be involved. Our kid will have a lot of love, which is more than I had."

I felt slapped in the face. "When did I ever not show you love?"

"I'm not talking about you, Mom."

"Brandon," I said, softening my tone. "If I could have forced your father to be more involved in your life, I would have."

"Right," he said blandly. "Look, I'll talk to you later."

Brandon hung up and I paced for a few moments, as my mind absorbed everything he'd told me. I cringed wondering if the three of them were going to sleep in the same bed. His new living arrangement was an embarrassment that I could never divulge to a soul. Ava had somehow managed to whip Brandon into a frenzy of such devotion that he would comply with any request she made, no matter how unconventional or bizarre.

However, looking on the bright side, he was safe, had a roof over his head, and apparently he was happy. He had plans to get a job—not obtain money selling drugs or in some other illegal way as I'd feared. I had to learn how to let go of Brandon. He was on his own life's path and there was nothing I could do to protect him from the innumerable mistakes he was bound to make along the way.

I told myself that from now on, I'd be emotionally supportive of him, but I would keep my opinions to myself. I only wished he wasn't so determined to bring a child into the chaotic life he was choosing to live.

Deciding to take my mind off Brandon, I glanced down at my phone and swiped to Jeff's text. I read it again and this time I smiled and tapped the keyboard on the screen with a response.

I'd love to go sailing. Is there anything you'd like me to bring?

I waited for his next text and was startled when my phone jingled in my hand.

"Hello?" I said questioningly. Jeff seemed to be so big on texting, I thought perhaps he'd tapped the call button by mistake.

"Hi, there. I hope I'm not interrupting you at work." His velvety smooth voice delighted all my senses. Realizing that he'd called intentionally put me in a good mood.

"No, you're not interrupting. I'm actually at home. I left work early today."

"Is everything all right?" The concern in his voice was endearing.

"Yes, everything is good. I took some personal time to run some errands." I found myself smiling and twirling several strands of hair. Jeff brought out a girlish side that I didn't realize still existed.

"Good to know you're okay. Well, in response to your question, the boat is fully stocked, and the only thing you need to bring is your lovely self and a swimsuit."

I frowned as I envisioned myself in swimwear. I wasn't overweight by any means; in fact I could stand to gain a few pounds. But being sedentary most of the time, I was a little jiggly in certain places, and I doubted if I was swimsuit ready. But a cover-up would hide any flaws. I desperately needed some fun in my life, and I wouldn't have missed the sailing date for anything in the world.

"The sailing time from the marina to Cape May is about four to five hours depending on the current, so we should leave at around five in the morning. I hope that's not too early for you."

"No, I'm an early riser."

"Great! Should I pick you up or would you prefer to meet me at the marina?"

Jeff was so accommodating and such a gentleman, but I couldn't invite him inside. My home, which I'd gotten in the divorce, along with a cabin in the Pocono Mountains, was quite lovely except for the gaping hole in the dining room. I hadn't bothered to get the wall fixed because I was too embarrassed to call Mr. Herbert, the handyman I always called to repair the destruction that Brandon caused. But with Brandon out of the house, this would be the absolute last time I'd have to use Mr. Herbert's services.

"Yes, you can pick me up at home. Thank you," I said gaily and then gave him my address.

After I hung up, I actually squealed and spun around in joy. Jeff was turning into my knight in shining armor, appearing in my life and rescuing me during one of my lowest points.

Realizing there were no certainties in romantic relationships, I refused to get my hopes up. It wasn't likely that Jeff and I would ride off into the sunset or live happily ever after. And although I dared not hope for anything serious and long term, I was perfectly content to take it moment-by-moment, allowing myself to enjoy every step of the way.

Chapter 8

I'd bought new clothes and accessories for the trip to Cape May. A tropical-print sundress, sandals with dangling seashells, and I'd gone to the salon and had my dull brown hair jazzed up with reddish-gold highlights. A silk flower headband added whimsy to my look. I was definitely in touch with my femininity. However, I wasn't looking forward to changing into the swimsuit that was packed in my carry-on bag. I was going to have to start doing some toning exercises to feel more confident around Jeff with his rock-hard body.

Overall, I felt prettier and more desirable than I had in years. Especially when he reached for my hand as we walked along the wood planks of the marina.

"There she is," he said with pride, pointing to a glorious white boat that glimmered in the rising sun.

"It's bigger than I imagined," I murmured in awe. "It looks more like a yacht than a regular sailboat."

"It is a yacht. It's a thirty-five-foot cruiser," Jeff clarified with pride in his tone. As we grew closer, I saw that *Allegra* was lettered in gilt on the hull.

"How sweet to name your boat after your daughter. I bet that made her feel special."

He shrugged. "You know kids. The day I showed her the boat, she seemed impressed at first, but the occasion turned out to be nothing more than an opportunity for her to take selfies as she struck poses in front of her name," Jeff said with laughter. "When I suggested we take her out on the water, Allegra was appalled. The idea of being stuck with her Dad and possibly have to make conversation for longer than five minutes didn't go over well with her." He chuckled and shook his head. "But had I allowed her to invite her new boyfriend and a group of their friends and if I promised to stick to steering the boat and stay out of their hair, she would have been ecstatic. Allegra's a difficult kid...hard to please. But that doesn't stop me from trying to get closer."

"Aw." I soothed and briskly rubbed his arm. But I couldn't help from thinking that Jeff had no idea what a difficult child was. An hour spent with Brandon would make him view Allegra as a perfect teen.

"What's your relationship like with your son? Are you two close?" he asked.

"We used to be when he was younger, but he started becoming more and more withdrawn after puberty." I spoke softly, solemnly, unable to conceal the sorrow that crept into my tone.

"If it's any consolation, I hear they open up a lot more and actually become likable people after they become adults. I have five years to go, but at least your son is almost there."

"Yeah, that's true," I said solemnly. It wasn't likely Brandon would mature anytime soon, and I was reminded of the unwise choices he was making and how hell-bent he was on ruining his young life.

Noticing that my mood had become somber, Jeff intuitively changed the subject. "We couldn't have asked for a more beautiful day to take the boat out, huh?" He flashed his gorgeous smile and my disposition instantly brightened.

"Let me show you around," he offered after ushering me on board. While taking a stroll around the interior of the roomy vessel with its exquisite modern design, it occurred to me that Jeff was certainly not a struggling entrepreneur. His consulting business must have been raking in the dough.

There was plush furniture all around, including sparkling top-of-the-line appliances and a rich mahogany dining table in the galley. Below deck were two cabins, smartly decorated as if by Martha Stewart herself. Stylish furniture, beautiful bedding, and the scent of fresh-cut flowers added to the elegant ambiance.

"I could live on this boat," I said wistfully.

"I spent lots of nights here before Allegra arrived for the summer. In order to keep a close eye on her, I have to be mindful of getting back home at a reasonable hour after a day of sailing. But I have no regrets," he quickly added. "Reconnecting with my daughter and focusing on parenting is what's most important right now."

I squeezed his arm in understanding. Though I was sure that Jeff could have had his pick of women who were prettier, more sophisticated and more successful than me, I was beginning to believe that our strained relationships with our offspring had unconsciously drawn us together. Maybe in time I'd be able to open up more about Brandon. It would be such a relief to be able to discuss what I was going through without the fear of judgment.

Jeff opened the fridge and pulled out a beer. "Want one?"

I wrinkled my nose. "Never developed a taste for beer."

"Right, you like those umbrella drinks. I'll whip up a batch of something tropical to match your dress. How does a Piña Colada sound?"

"Sounds great."

"Good. I'll make us drinks and then prepare something for us to eat after we get out on the water."

"No, you've got enough to handle with navigating the boat. Let me make myself useful by fixing a meal and preparing the drinks."

"I can't argue against teamwork." Jeff gave me a quick peck on the cheek and went up to the cockpit.

Since I rarely cooked and subsisted on takeout, opening the fridge or the kitchen cabinets at home was bound to be depressing. But peering into the fridge on Jeff's boat was a sheer delight. There were numerous beverage choices, cold cuts, an assortment of cheeses, fresh fruit and veggies, all sorts of gourmet condiments, various cuts of meat, and two large lobster tails were wrapped in cellophane. Impressive!

Not having the foggiest idea how to make a Pina Colada, I used my phone to go online and track down a recipe. Amazingly, Jeff had every required ingredient, including heavy whipping cream and fresh pineapple.

One-by-one I dumped the ingredients in the blender and turned it on. After pouring the batch into a pitcher, I began making sandwiches, humming as I layered slices of turkey breast. When I heard the rumble of the engine and felt the boat begin to glide, it dawned on me that I couldn't recall the last time I'd felt so relaxed and content.

Already, I was having a wonderful time, and the date had barely gotten started.

When we reached the New Jersey coast, we docked and took a quick swim. Afterward, I was so relaxed and at ease, I completely forgot about my issue with my thighs. Perhaps I'd been overly critical because they looked perfectly fine and didn't require a cover-up. Wearing my damp swimsuit, I stood next to Jeff on deck looking out at the water.

Jeff's sun-bronzed shoulders and broad chest were dotted with glimmering droplets of water that looked like diamonds. God, he was so hot, scandalous thoughts began swirling in my head, and I had to take a deep sip of my drink to cool off.

"This is the life," I said, looking up at him with an innocent smile that I hoped disguised the lust that was welling inside. "Thanks for inviting me."

"Thanks for joining me on such short notice. It would be nice to be able to get away for longer than a day trip and take in the nightlife here at the shore."

"Sounds lovely. Let me know when and I'll make myself available." I moved closer to him, enjoying the feeling of being anchored by his hard body while the boat gently rocked back and forth.

"How about next weekend? I'm pretty sure I can get a sitter for Allegra." We both laughed at the absurdity of him getting a sitter for his teenager who looked like a full-grown woman. "Seriously, I can make arrangements with her friend's parents. Believe me, Allegra won't object to having me out of her hair." He wrapped an arm around me and when I nestled my head against his shoulder, he pressed his lips against my wet hair. It was such a sweet gesture, giving me a feeling of being cocooned in masculine warmth and protection.

Back inside the boat, we went to separate cabins and changed out of our damp swimwear. I took my time freshening up, putting on a little makeup, and blow-drying my hair. When I emerged, Jeff was in the galley wearing a chef's apron. He had pans going on the stove while he chopped and diced vegetables.

"What are you making? Can I help?" I asked, even though I wasn't a very good cook.

"I'm making lobster-stuffed filet mignon and all I want you to do is sit back and relax."

"Aye, aye, captain." I gave him a little salute and helped myself to another cocktail while he moved around the space turning down burners, measuring ingredients, and sprinkling salt and pepper over the food that sizzled on top of the stove.

I was flooded with waves of awe and happiness as I watched him hard at work, preparing a meal for us. If someone had told me a few weeks ago that I would be sailing on a beautiful boat and being pampered in this manner, I wouldn't have believed it could be even remotely possible.

While we were eating, I told Jeff all about my dreadful marriage, Howard's disdain for our son, and how it had affected Brandon. Jeff frowned and uttered in disgust that Howard was a heartless bastard. I divulged how I'd spoiled Brandon, ruined him actually, in an attempt to compensate for his father's lack of love.

"You did the best you could," he said consolingly.

By the time I finished pouring out my heart, I felt lighter. Like a Catholic must feel after confessing to a priest. Maybe it was the rum in the Piña Coladas that had loosened me up, but I told myself it was Jeff—the way he put me at ease.

After we'd loaded the dishwasher, I found myself taking Jeff by the hand and leading him to the cabin that had been designated as mine. I'd never been an aggressive woman, yet I found myself advancing toward the bed.

Then Jeff took the lead, kissing me tenderly as he undressed me, and then growing more passionate, fisting my hair in his hands. My body was burning up, heat scorching me from the inside out. He guided me down to a supine position and I watched shamelessly as he tore off his clothes, my eyes taking in his beautiful body as if trying to commit to memory every rippling muscle.

His hands roamed over my buttocks and then moved upward and around to my breasts, squeezing them gently, his hot fingers nearly searing my flesh.

His mouth caressed my ear. "I want you, Claire," he whispered as he touched me in secret places, filling me with an ache that twisted in my belly like a claw and pulsating within my very core. I sighed long and loud as his tongue lashed against my breasts, causing my body temperature to climb even higher. I could feel my nipples tightening beneath the warm wet slide of his tongue, while at the same time, his thumb brushed against the firm bud between my thighs.

My body shook and I cried out his name in a desperate plea for him to end the aching torture. Accommodating my desire, Jeff mounted me. Clinging to him, I whimpered in gratitude as I arched my back and spread my legs in invitation.

Chapter 9

Setting up for the department's Monday morning staff meeting, Veronica had laid out an array of bagels, donuts, cookies, and steaming coffee on the sideboard. On the table next to it were folders, Sharpies, and stacks of printed materials.

"Good morning, Veronica," I greeted breezily when I arrived.

Veronica did a double-take. "Well, look at you! Your tan is beautiful. What did you do—spend the entire weekend lying on the beach reading romance novels?"

"That would have been nice," I replied. "Actually, I spent most of the weekend in my backyard, spray-painting a chair I picked up at a thrift store."

Veronica raised a brow. "You spray-painted fabric?"

"It's a new trend. The modern way of reupholstering. I found the instructions on a YouTube video."

A look of annoyance crossed Veronica's face. "Well, I wouldn't know anything about YouTube, MyTube, HisTube or anything else connected with that blasted Internet. Watching cable TV with a remote in my hand is trendy enough for me."

Veronica was the only employee in my department—in the entire company for that matter—that wasn't computer literate, which was one of the reasons upper management had tried to get rid of her. She was a dinosaur who insisted on doing all of her paperwork by hand, leaving the task of inputting her information into the system to either me or one of the members of my staff. It was a pain, but nevertheless, she was an invaluable employee.

Although I considered her a friend, I wasn't ready to tell her about my newfound romantic interest. I could hardly believe it myself and I didn't want to jinx the relationship by putting labels on it too soon. Until I was confident that Jeff and I were exclusive, it would be my little secret.

Veronica glanced at me skeptically. "Are you sure all you did was spray-paint a chair?"

"Positive. Why do you ask?"

"You have a glow about you, and you seem a lot happier than you've been in quite a while. Even though your new hobby sounds a little bonkers, I'm glad you found something that takes your focus off that troubled boy of yours. Speaking of Brandon, how's he doing?"

I shrugged. "He's pretty much the same...as far as his temperament."

She gazed at me over her reading glasses. "So you still haven't laid down the law with him, have you?"

I swallowed. My first reaction was to become defensive, but I reminded myself that Brandon was on his own path and I was on mine. "Oh, there is some good news about Brandon. He has a lead on a job, so my fingers are crossed that it'll work out for him," I said brightly. "But even if it doesn't, I give him credit for at least making an effort to look for employment."

Unimpressed, Veronica snorted and mumbled something indistinct. From her attitude, I could tell she thought I was still coddling him. She had no idea that Brandon had moved out and I didn't intend to tell her. Sharing the intimate details of his new life would encourage her to make a judgmental comment, and she'd be particularly harsh and critical if she were aware of the disturbing love triangle that Brandon was involved in.

Staff began trickling in and heading straight for the high-carb, sugary spread. As they congregated around the sideboard, slathering cream cheese and butter on bagels, Veronica nudged me.

"By the way, that new volunteer, Walter, is a pretty decent fellow."

"Does that mean he's following your rules and regulations to the letter?" I teased, knowing how bossy Veronica could be.

"Oh, he tried to take over at first. Can you believe he tried to show me the proper way to repot a philodendron? But after I gave him an extended sidelong glance, he had sense enough to back off."

I laughed, imagining the look Veronica had given him.

"He's a widower," she said in a confidential tone.

"Oh?"

"The wife died a year ago, right after he'd retired. They lived in a fancy apartment in the city, but after she passed, he found himself yearning for the feeling of grass beneath his feet and being surrounded by nature. He'd always been good with houseplants, but was ready to take up gardening, so he moved to our beautiful little town."

I wanted to tell her that Jeff had also recently moved here, but I stopped myself. If Veronica had any idea that Jeff and I were dating, she'd bug me every day with intrusive questions about our relationship. My instincts told me to stay mum on the subject.

"You won't believe how I spent Saturday," she said, her face flushing slightly.

I held out my hands. "Bouldering?" We both laughed. Mentioning a sport that Jeff enjoyed was as close as I was willing to get on the topic of my handsome lover.

And what a lover he was. Recalling the way his hands had gone from soft caresses to squeezing me passionately made me feel woozy.

"You'll never guess, so I might as well tell you," Veronica said, cutting into my erotic thoughts. "On Saturday I did some bird watching with Walter."

"Bird watching?" I repeated, making a face. "You went bird watching with the volunteer?"

"There's nothing in the company handbook that says you can't strike up a friendship outside of work with a volunteer," she responded.

"I know. I'm just surprised, that's all." And I was also a little disheartened. I couldn't get rid of Walter as I'd planned now that he and Veronica had struck up a friendship. I wondered if he'd subjected her to his continuous winking and tongue-clicking or if that was something he reserved for younger women.

"As boring as bird watching may sound, it was a lot of fun. It may not have been as much fun without Walter, but I had a surprisingly good time. By the way, I invited Walter to join us at salsa class. You don't mind, do you?"

I minded very much, but said, "No, not at all." Seeing Walter on the job twice a week and then again at salsa class was too much of Winking Walter for me. I hadn't mentioned it to Veronica, but I'd already planned on quitting my salsa instructions. I wasn't comfortable with the idea of bumping into Jeff at the center. After our romantic date on Saturday, we'd spent Sunday talking on the phone off and on, and texting throughout the day. I was quickly becoming attached to him and had no idea how I'd handle it emotionally if I saw him conversing with another woman at the community center.

Sleeping with him took things to another level, and I'd probably become jealous and suspicious if I caught him even looking at another woman.

Furthermore, I wasn't comfortable with the idea of interacting with his daughter, Allegra, during salsa class. Though I would never divulge my impressions of his daughter to Jeff, I found her to be an unlikable young lady—extremely haughty and vain.

And with Brandon's mumbled way of speaking and hostile attitude, it wasn't likely that Jeff would be a fan of his, either. I figured it was best if we left our unpleasant offspring out of the equation for as long as possible. When and if the time came when Brandon's and Allegra's inclusion in our lives was unavoidable, then Jeff and I would endure their insufferable behavior together. Hopefully, when that day came, Brandon would have come to his senses and gotten rid of Ava. He was difficult enough to contend with on his own, but if he brought along trashy Ava and possibly her other lover, Muffy, as well ...it would be simply too much to unleash upon polite company.

I called the meeting to order and the staffers, comprised of five women and two men, reluctantly tore themselves away from the pastries and took seats at the conference table. The rickety and nicked conference table was a hand-me-down from another department at the zoo whose budget included more upscale office furniture.

The meeting had just gotten underway when I mentioned that I needed to assign someone to the position of recycling coordinator of Zoo-Doo. Zoo-Doo was the cutesy name that had been given to the zoo's compost project. Until now, Meghan had overseen the project, but with her recent promotion came new responsibilities.

At the mere mention of Zoo-Doo, everyone at the table suddenly cast their glances downward. Some became interested in their fingernails, others fiddled with coffee stirrers, and Dwight Evans, usually a loudmouth at meetings, became uncharacteristically quiet and focused his attention on straightening out a paper clip.

No one would make eye contact with me and I understood their discomfort.

Our zoo created nearly one million pounds of compost each year and saved $50,000 per year in disposable costs, yet my department didn't have a decent conference table.

The one hundred percent recycled product was an exotic blend of animal manures mixed with straw, grass, leaves and wood chips from the grounds of the zoo.

Although zoo officials, environmentalists, and Go-green fanatics were proud of Zoo-Doo, my staffers loathed having to steer a wheelbarrow filled with excrement that was collected from giraffe, hippos, gazelles, and zebras, among other non-primate herbivore animals.

Veronica winced and rubbed her left hip. "My doctor still has me on light duty. Pushing around that blasted wheel barrel would aggravate my condition."

"Why don't we rotate on a monthly basis," I suggested. "Dwight, you can start it off."

Dwight dropped the unfurled paper clip. As if he'd been shot in the chest, he fell against the back of his chair. He was so obnoxious and dramatic.

"How am I supposed to deal with my regular responsibilities and go around collecting shit twice a day," Dwight complained.

My phone suddenly vibrated, rattling loudly against the wooden table. I peeked at the screen and was surprised to see that the call was from Brandon.

"I have to take this," I said, making an apologetic face. Since it wasn't the norm for Brandon to be up before noon, I assumed there was an emergency. I stood up abruptly. "I'll only be a second," I said as I moved hastily toward the door.

In the privacy of the corridor, I whispered frantically, "What's wrong, Brandon?"

"Nothing. Everything's great. I wanted to let you know that I interviewed for that factory job in Secane...and they hired me. I start tomorrow morning." I could hear a smile in his voice.

"That's fantastic, Brandon. I'm so proud of you," I said with a huge grin blossoming on my face.

"Thanks. Yo, Mom, I need a favor. I need to borrow some money. I'm on a different shift than Muffy, and I'm going to need money for the bus and other incidentals. They want me to wear non-skid black shoes and jeans aren't allowed. You have to wear black khakis."

"I can drop off some money after work today. Do you want me to stop by Ava's place or would you rather meet me somewhere?"

"You can drop it off here." He gave me the address and then advised me to honk the horn when I arrived.

"How much do you need?"

"For the work clothes and bus fare until I get paid, I'd say, I need at least a hundred bucks."

"Okay, I'll stop at the ATM on my way. Congrats, hon. I'll see you this evening."

I returned to the meeting so elated over Brandon's news, one would have thought I'd been told he'd been accepted into Yale or Harvard. At twenty years old, my son was gainfully employed for the first time in his life.

But there was something else that warmed my heart. Brandon didn't sound troubled and he wasn't brooding. His tone was jubilant. My son actually sounded happy—an extremely rare emotion for him.

Maybe Ava wasn't such a bad influence after all. I made a mental note to be more cordial toward her from now on. Their arrangement was unconventional to say the least, but who was I to judge? Following the norms of society didn't ensure a lower divorce rate or well-adjusted children.

Back at the conference table, I was determined to maintain an air of quiet control though I was bursting with excitement. Although the discussion over Zoo-Doo had become heated, I didn't get involved. I was busy imagining Brandon getting promotions at his new job and advancing from a laborer to an executive of the company. If he applied himself and went back to school part time, it was entirely possible.

"In order to end all this bickering, I'll take on the responsibility of being the coordinator," Veronica offered, sounding like a martyr. "Is that okay with you, Claire?"

Hearing my name brought me out of my reverie.

Before I could collect my thoughts and respond, Dwight blurted, "What about your bad hip?" Then he leaned back and smirked at Veronica.

"As coordinator, I won't have to do any physical labor," she explained with a sly smile. "I'll create the schedule with the names of the staff that will actually scoop up the animal poop and the leaves, and everything. I'll list the dates that they're required to be on *Zoo-Poo* patrol." She gave a little laugh, but no one joined in.

"Make sure you don't put my name on the schedule," Meghan reminded her, pursing her lips with an air of self-importance.

"We're all well aware that you're moving up the ladder. Hopefully, you're not gunning for Claire's job," Veronica shot back, believing that her advanced age gave her the right to say anything that popped in her head.

Meghan's face flushed. "Why would you accuse me of that?"

"I've seen you hobnobbing with the big bosses, and I'm only checking," Veronica said, staring at Meghan over her glasses.

It hadn't occurred to me that Meghan wanted my job; she was much too young and inexperienced, but I'd have my guard up from now on. Perhaps it would behoove me to get a little chummy with the suit-wearing executives that ran the place behind the scenes.

Veronica cleared her throat. "So...I'll maintain the schedule and make sure the rotation flows smoothly." She glanced at me. "With Claire's permission, of course."

I smiled approvingly. "You have my permission."

Veronica had finally snagged a position of authority and I had no doubt she'd get the job done.

Chapter 10

My whirlwind affair with Jeff had been going on since the beginning of summer and by mid-August, we'd become inseparable. We sailed every weekend and his boat had become a second home to me. And we didn't limit our fun to the weekends only. During the week after work, we played miniature golf, attended jazz concerts and gallery openings, and I cheered Jeff on when he competed in trivia night contests at a local pub.

Although he was a newcomer to the East Coast, Jeff had made an astonishing amount of friends not only in the city where he conducted most of his business, but also in our small town. He was on a first-name basis with far more people in Middletown than me, and I'd been a resident for over twenty years.

It was almost magical the way I'd gone from a homebody to a social butterfly, and it was all Jeff's doing. Being out on the town with him, my arm looped inside his, gave me such a sense of pride and an overall feeling of well-being. I now realized that before him, I'd merely been existing—getting through each day as best I could. And now I was enjoying life to the fullest. Once a solemn introvert, I had morphed into a happy, outgoing person who smiled often and struck up conversations with strangers.

Though Jeff and I had never brought up the L-word nor had we bothered to identify exactly what we were doing, I'd never experienced such a feeling of wholeness. Had never imagined such blissful happiness even existed.

It was as if all the stars had aligned perfectly. Brandon was in a good place in his own life, and his stability and peace of mind allowed me to enjoy my new, romantic adventures—guilt free.

Oddly, my liaison with Jeff went unnoticed by Veronica. She was so busy conducting her own love affair with Walter, she wasn't paying any attention to me. I liked the new Veronica who was too preoccupied with her own life to pry into mine. It was refreshing not to have my parenting skills questioned on a regular basis.

She meant no harm, but she had a tendency to be extremely judgmental, which was why I hadn't told her about my relationship with Jeff. I didn't want her prying into my love life and badgering me with questions about a wedding date. Veronica had the antiquated notion that a couple should be engaged after dating six months and married no longer than a year after the engagement was announced.

I wondered if those rules applied to her and Walter's relationship—or were they exempt because of their advanced ages.

I also wondered if they were sexual. I couldn't picture it, but with the availability of male enhancement drugs, there was nothing preventing them from being intimate. She and Walter were the cutest couple, especially when they playfully bickered over the best bug sprays, topsoil versus potting soil, or the proper way to plant tomatoes. They were both know-it-alls when it came to horticulture.

Over time, Walter had grown on me and I no longer minded his presence in our department. He didn't seem to wink as much or maybe I didn't notice it anymore. Actually, he spent most of his time assisting Veronica in the greenhouse, and I didn't see him very often.

But what really won me over and warmed my heart toward Walter was the way he willingly pitched in and helped with Zoo-Doo and never once complained.

My life was so fantastic, I'd managed to get Brandon to comply with my desire for us to touch base at least once or twice a week. We didn't have lengthy phone conversations, nor did he initiate any discussions, but he spoke audibly and no longer mumbled half-hearted responses to my questions regarding his job and how things were working out at home.

I didn't feel comfortable visiting Brandon at the apartment with Ava and Muffy, but occasionally, I'd make arrangements to meet him at his job during his lunch break. During those visits, I'd slip him cash—pocket money so he'd be able to purchase the latest video game or other personal items for himself. I had kept him on my phone plan and continued to pay his phone bill. I enjoyed helping him out now that he was proving he could be a productive member of society.

Also, I felt bad for him. He was only making minimum wage and he turned most of his earnings over to Ava for household expenses. With Brandon finally being responsible, the last thing I wanted was for him to become disillusioned and frustrated over limited funds.

Once, when a flyer came in the mail announcing a comic book convention that was being held in the city, I surprised him with two tickets—one for him and one for either Ava or maybe a friend from work. I was working on being accepting, but I still wasn't so open-minded that I was willing to purchase tickets for him, Ava, *and* Muffy. Besides, I was sure he and Ava could use some alone time.

"Thanks, Mom," he had said when I gave him the tickets, beaming as he embraced me. Not one prone to displays of affection, Brandon's tight hug surprised and delighted me. I was doing everything I could to repair our fractured relationship, and amazingly, Brandon was cooperating.

As much as I disliked her, I had to admit that Ava deserved most of the credit for Brandon's transformation. In her own warped way, she was helping to make a man out of my son.

Jeff and I were browsing antique shops. Antiques weren't my thing, but Jeff had a way of making everything fun. I enjoyed listening to him haggling over the price of a vintage radio. After Jeff got the owner to agree to a price of his liking, we went to celebrate the victory at a sidewalk café.

"Wouldn't it be great to do this in Paris?" he asked after we'd been served baguettes and coffee.

"This feels like Paris to me," I said, gesturing at the sidewalk that was jammed with tables and chairs and throngs of merry people.

"This doesn't begin to compare to the real Paris. It's awesome, and you'd love it."

"Maybe I'll see it one day."

"I think you should see Paris sooner than later."

Intrigued, I leaned forward. "How soon?"

"Next week."

I nearly choked. "You're not serious," I said, laughing.

"Oh, but I am," he said, smiling and nodding and looking even more handsome than ever if that were possible.

"What about Allegra?"

"She's leaving tomorrow."

"What! I thought she was staying until after Labor Day."

"Yeah, that was the original plan, but she had a breakup with her boyfriend who lives in Middletown, and then she made up with her ex who lives in L.A., and now she can't wait to get out of here and refuses to stay another day." He gave a shrug. "She's a fickle kid. I can't lock her in her room and force her to stay."

"Wow, I never got to know her. I figured there was plenty of time," I said sadly.

"Hey, don't look so glum. She'll be back during Christmas break, and hopefully by then, I'll have established a relationship with Brandon, and we'll all be ready to become a happy blended family."

"Family? What exactly are you saying?"

"I'm saying you make me happy. I want to be with you all the time...and I love you."

Stunned, I covered my mouth with my hand. After getting my bearings, I mouthed the words, "I love you, too," as I looked around embarrassedly, wondering if anyone had overheard our intimate conversation.

"Paris is for lovers, you know. So, how about it? We'll explore the most romantic city in the world for seven whole days." He flashed me another charming smile.

I hadn't had a real vacation since the days when Brandon was a teen and we would go to our cabin in the mountains. The past few years, I'd always gone to the cabin alone and typically only stayed two or three days at the most.

"Well?" Jeff asked insistently.

"I don't have a passport," I admitted, holding up my hands in defeat.

"That's not a problem. We can get your application expedited for a small additional fee."

"It's all so sudden. I'm not sure."

"You only live once, Claire. What do you say?"

"Okay, let's do it," I said with false bravado. As I spoke I could picture my boss at work balking loudly at my bad timing and then grunting in disapproval as he reluctantly granted my request for a spur-of-the-moment vacation.

Jeff leaned across the table and kissed me. "We're going to have the time of our lives. When we return, I want to meet Brandon and spend time with him. I know you said he's only interested in video games and comics, but I bet I could get him interested in golfing.

Real golf, not the putt-putt stuff you and I fool around with," he said, referring to miniature golf.

I doubted if Brandon would agree to play golf with Jeff. Not even virtual golf, his preferred format for all sports. It wasn't likely that Brandon would be interested in the least in becoming acquainted with Jeff. I feared that forcing Brandon to interact with his mother's love interest might be so unexpected and jolting, he might lapse back into his old reclusive and hostile personality.

It was time to tell Jeff about Brandon—time to explain that my son was *different*. And that he was very fragile. It was also time to divulge to Jeff that Brandon didn't live at home and was determined to conceive a child that he planned to raise with a pair of lesbians. Brandon's situation was so embarrassing, I had no idea how to broach the subject.

Procrastinating, I decided to wait and tell him after we returned from Paris. I had a nagging fear that Jeff might have a change of heart about our relationship after he met my antisocial son and learned about his unusual lifestyle.

I couldn't blame Jeff if he couldn't picture Ava and Muffy being a part of his vision of a happy, blended family.

Chapter 11

With Allegra back in Los Angeles with her mother, I began staying at Jeff's place several nights during the week. Our lovemaking on the boat had always been sweet and satisfying, but he became an even more intense and adventurous lover within the confines of his own home.

He was insatiable, and the moment I walked in the door, he'd start tearing off my clothes. Most nights we never made it upstairs. We'd end up on the floor of the foyer, the living room, or at the bottom of the staircase, making ferocious love. Our sex life had become almost animalistic in its intensity...and I loved every second of it.

This kind of unbridled passion was something I'd never had and at forty-two, I was in my sexual prime and couldn't get enough. We were addicted to each other. Sex went on for hours at night and resumed in the morning before we left for work.

The days leading up to our trip to Paris went by in a blur. There was so much shopping to do. The luggage I used for business trips simply wasn't suitable for a romantic getaway of this caliber, and I ended up spending an outrageous amount of money on three pieces of luggage.

I was spending so much more than I normally did in an attempt to look like the sophisticated, fashionable woman that a man like Jeff would have on his arm. I hadn't seen any photos of his ex-wife, but I imagined her being someone with an elegant sense of style.

One day during my lunch break, I went to a med-spa for a little Botox to even out the fine lines that I was beginning to notice on my face. I'd never been a vain person, but being in love influenced me to strive to always look my best.

Since I'd started seeing Jeff, I spent more time at the beauty salon than ever before. I was constantly getting my hair tinted to keep the gray strands at bay. No longer satisfied with my mom panties and bras, I spent a ton of money on expensive lingerie that cost more than I'd spend on a winter coat.

But my efforts didn't go unnoticed by Jeff. He constantly complimented me. And his approval was worth the extra time I put into my appearance and the extra money I'd spent.

I still dressed the same at work, wearing clothes purchased from T.J. Maxx and Target, but I had slowly begun to accumulate a much more fashionable and costly wardrobe for my numerous dates with Jeff.

Jeff had exquisite taste in everything from food to the high-end designer socks he wore. He enjoyed luxuries. Once, when spotting a credit card receipt tossed on his bureau, I couldn't resist taking a look. I literally gasped when I realized that he'd spent seven hundred dollars on a haircut at a fancy salon in the city.

Maybe that was why his silver hair had such a rich glimmer to it and always looked stylishly moussed.

And although we never discussed it, money, I assumed, was not a concern of Jeff's.

I didn't want us to appear as an ill-matched couple, prompting people to wonder what he saw in me, and so I had started reading *Vogue* and other fashion magazines, from cover-to-cover, as if adhering to their beauty guidelines was the key to securing my relationship with Jeff.

I'd gotten so attached to him, so quickly that the thought of losing him terrified me. Luckily, our feelings for each other were mutual. We were equally crazy about each other, calling and texting throughout the day, both eager to get home and rip each other's clothes off.

We didn't go out after work during the week leading up to Paris. And I didn't care if we never went on another romantic date again. Merely being in his presence was enough for me. His sweet kisses and passionate lovemaking were the icing on the cake.

Although I doubted that he'd invited me to Paris to propose, I was pretty certain that he was going to ask me to move in with him. And the answer was going to be a resounding yes!

As for Brandon, he still didn't know about Jeff and me. I told him I had to take a work trip—another horticulture convention. Then I gave him back his house key, just in case something happened while I was away and he needed to come home.

He looked at the key and without any expression or words of thanks, he stuffed it in his pocket. Despite his lack of outward joy, I could tell he liked the security of having it back.

"You look nice, Mom," Brandon exclaimed, as if noticing for the first time that my appearance had changed from drab to attractive.

"Thanks, hon. I'm going to miss you while I'm gone, but I'm going to call you every day, so don't duck my calls," I said teasingly.

"I won't." He sounded offended.

"I know you wouldn't. I was only kidding," I explained. Brandon had never had a sense of humor, and sadly he wasn't likely to acquire one. He was missing that gene. But I'd take his lack of humor any day over the hostile, disgruntled person he used to be.

Filled with an overwhelming sense of gratitude, I hugged my boy and rustled his curly hair. I was so proud of him—proud of both of us for putting forth the effort to finally figure out how to heal our badly damaged relationship.

I love you, I said in my mind. Saying the words out loud would have made Brandon uncomfortable, causing him to stare at the ground and shift from foot-to-foot. He'd only recently started allowing me to hug him, so I had to be cautious and not overwhelm him with too much affection.

I was certain that his inability to show me any warmth or affection stemmed from his father's rejection of him. I wondered how he was with Ava. Did they kiss and cuddle or did she merely use him for stud services?

Catching myself engaging in negative thinking about Ava, I quickly reminded myself that Brandon was happy. Still, as much as I tried to think kinder thoughts about Ava, in the back of my mind, I was hoping and praying that my son would never conceive a child with her. No child deserved to come into the world as a result of such a heinous union.

"I can't believe you've never flown first-class," Jeff teased as we reclined in our spacious seats on the plane. "Your ex is one of the wealthiest men in Middletown, and I find it hard to believe that you two flew coach when you were together."

"Howard was building his business back then. He wasn't the real estate tycoon that he is today. As I told you, all I got out of the divorce was the house, a cabin in the mountains, and child support for Brandon."

"That sucks," he said solemnly.

"Here you go," said the young flight attendant with a toothy smile as she brought us glasses of wine. Being extra solicitous toward Jeff, she arranged his napkin carefully before setting the base of the glass upon it. She was a bit more lax with the service she provided me. I chuckled to myself when I noticed that my napkin was slightly askew.

Jeff thanked her and then returned his attention to me, asking how I liked the Cabernet Franc.

"It's good," I said, taking another sip and smiling to myself when I noticed the disappointment on the face of the flight attendant when she realized that she'd been dismissed.

Jeff's attentiveness to me was one of the many things that I adored about him. From waitresses to art gallery owners, women threw themselves at him everywhere we went, and though always polite and friendly, he never behaved in a manner that would cause me discomfort.

In fact, it was almost as if he was oblivious to the women who shamelessly flaunted themselves in an attempt to get his attention. Consistently, he proved that he only had eyes for me.

I should have been bursting with pride and joy, but instead of basking in his love and fully enjoying the exciting life I was sharing with him, I was constantly worrying and fretting. I was plagued with negative thoughts and the belief that our affair was too good to be true. I secretly harbored the fear that one day Jeff would wake up and wonder what he'd ever seen in such an uninteresting person like me.

To me, Jeff was like an extraordinary birthday gift that I was allowed to admire and enjoy for only a limited time, and then the wonderful present had to be returned to the store.

Sorrow suddenly engulfed me. No matter how good of a time we had in Paris, it was inevitable that sooner or later Jeff was going to grow bored with me.

Howard certainly had, and he wasn't nearly as handsome, athletic, and charismatic as Jeff.

Jeff leaned over and kissed me on the cheek.

"What was that for?" I inquired, unable to suppress a proud smile.

"For indulging me and agreeing to accompany me to Paris on such short notice."

"Only a fool would say no to a dream vacation with a hot stud like you," I replied, my face flushing slightly. Playful banter that included sexual innuendos was not something that I was accustomed to. But ever since Jeff and I had started seeing each other, I'd loosened up considerably. I wasn't nearly as reserved as I used to be. Especially not in bed.

Thinking about our heated lovemaking sessions made me want to grab a magazine from the pouch in front of me and use it to fan myself. But thoughts of lust quickly turned to deep sorrow. He wanted to meet Brandon when we got back, and Brandon didn't present well. He was awkward around strangers and often compensated for his shyness by being hostile and rude.

"What's on your mind?" Jeff asked. "You seem pensive, all of a sudden. Hope you're not having second thoughts about Paris."

"Not at all. I'm wondering if I should pinch myself and find out if this has all been a dream."

"It's real, Claire. That's why I want to get acquainted with Brandon and meet your other family members. You've never said much about your relatives—not even your parents."

This wasn't the conversation I wanted to have on the way to our dream vacation, but I didn't want to create any tension between us by saying that I'd rather not talk about my family.

Preparing to indulge his curiosity, I took in a deep breath. "Well, my dad died when I was in middle school. He was driving. He was on his way to work when he had a massive heart attack. Eyewitnesses said the car continued moving for quite a while, going through stop signs and red lights, with a dead man behind the wheel."

"Oh, man. That's horrible. Sweetheart, I'm so sorry I brought it up." Jeff put an arm around me consolingly.

"It's okay, Jeff. I tend to keep unpleasant memories bottled up, but I probably need to be more open."

"When you're ready. I can tell that the topic is causing you distress."

"It is. But I need to get it out." I swallowed. "After my dad died, my mom discovered that my dad hadn't left us any money. He'd stopped making life insurance payments and had gambled away my college fund. She had to take on part-time work in addition to her full-time job to pay the bills. Over time she became resentful of me. She also started drinking. Once, in the midst of a drunken rage, she blurted that she'd only had me to placate my father and now he was gone and she was stuck with me."

A look of outrage covered Jeff's face. "What kind of mother would say something so hurtful to a child?"

"Needless to say, we had a strained relationship. But we learned to put up with each other. After Howard divorced me, I became ill and had to have minor surgery. I had no choice but to ask my mom to help me with Brandon while I recovered.

"I caught her drinking while she was supposed to be taking care of him. I shouted at her and called her irresponsible and she responded by saying that having to look after an autistic child was like caring for a zombie.

"She even suggested that he was missing a chromosome. She stuck the knife in deeper by saying that she didn't blame my ex for leaving me and a messed-up kid like Brandon."

"Oh, man," Jeff said, shaking his head. "How come you never mentioned that Brandon was autistic?"

"Because he's not," I said in a voice raised higher than I'd intended. "He just different," I explained in a lowered voice. "He's awkward around people and prefers to keep to himself. He's a brooder. A really unhappy young man. But he's getting better."

Jeff patted my hand. "Hey, let's drop the subject. I already dig your kid because I love you. I'll learn his ways and make sure to give him his space."

"There's more to it," I mumbled, not making eye contact. "He moved in with this really tacky girl, and I'm trying to be accepting because more than anything, I want my son to be happy..." On the verge of tears, my voice caught and I couldn't continue.

"It's okay, babe. As parents, we have to learn to let go. Even when we fear our kids are making horrible mistakes, it's their road to travel and we can't walk it for them."

I was sniffling, dabbing at my eyes with the napkin that had been beneath my drink, and smiling at the same time.

I had no idea what I'd done to deserve such a wonderful, understanding man like Jeff, but I knew with certainty that I was going to hold on to his love with everything I had.

Chapter 12

Paris! The entire city was a gorgeous setting of historic monuments and scenic bridges over the Seine River and the fashionably dressed Parisians were delightful to observe. Even though I could only understand a few French words, listening to the beautiful language soothed my soul.

Jeff was right about the French café back home. It couldn't begin to compete with the real thing. On our first evening in Paris, we dined at a crowded café that was located in a cobblestone alley.

It was utterly charming. There was nothing more intimate than being seated amidst a sea of round wooden tables. We were all so closely crammed together, our elbows knocked into the people on either side of us. We laughed with the other patrons and shared a bottle of Burgundy and a platter of cheese and charcuterie as we waited for our main courses. And when the wine began to take effect, Jeff and I couldn't stop stealing kisses right there at the table.

The evening was divine.

During our seven-day stay, Jeff and I spent long days exploring the city and its popular attractions and we spent even longer nights in our hotel room making love with wild abandon until the sun came up.

I enjoyed visiting the famous Louvre art museum, the Eiffel Tower, Luxembourg Gardens, and other popular tourist attractions, but I could have been just as happy if we never left our hotel room and stayed in bed all day.

Once, during a full-day winery tour, where we discovered the pleasures and history of champagne, we literally walked for hours. During the seven-hour tour, we visited the house of Moët & Chandon, which boasted seventeen miles of wine cellars. We also stopped by the gravesite of Dom Perignon, and I was surprised to learn that the father of the French bubbly had been a monk.

Tramping through the vines in the fields was no walk in the park for me. It was a scorching hot day and I was being eaten alive by unusual-looking bugs. Dust swirled around, coating my skin and sticking to my hair, and my feet were killing me. But Jeff was having such a wonderful time, I didn't utter a word of complaint.

In the course of the day, we learned the different techniques for growing and harvesting champagne. I'd never tasted so much champagne in my life, and by midday I was extra giggly and staggering so badly I had to hold on to Jeff's arm to keep my balance.

By the end of the ridiculously long tour, I was itchy, sweaty, and felt like I was covered in grit and grime. All I wanted to do was get back to the hotel and take a hot bath and go to bed. I was so terribly exhausted, I was willing to forgo a steamy night of amazing sex.

But Jeff had other plans.

"I have a surprise for you," he said as I ran my bathwater.

"Nooo, I don't want a surprise. All I want to do is relax in a tub of hot scented water."

"Sorry. You have to bathe quickly; we have an appointment in thirty minutes."

"An appointment to do what?" The thought of traipsing around Paris instead of getting badly needed rest was so upsetting, my voice went up several pitches.

"You'll find out. Now hurry, my love. Wash up quickly."

My skin was still damp as he hustled me out of our room and escorted me to the elevator. "Where're we going, Jeff?" I asked in irritation as the elevator ascended.

But Jeff's only response was a mysterious smile.

When the doors opened, we stepped out onto the floor of the hotel's luxurious spa.

Instead of giving me the traditional box of chocolates, Jeff pampered me with a decadent, "All About Chocolate" spa treatment. He kissed me on the cheek before leaving me in the capable hands of the spa staff.

A chocolate-body scrub was followed by a Swiss chocolate and toffee body wrap, and finished up with a deep tissue massage using cocoa oil. It was the most relaxing experience of my life. After two hours of pure, chocolate bliss—without the extra calories—I was left with the wonderful sensation of floating on a cloud.

The rest of the days were filled with shopping trips, visiting tourist attractions, and dining in elegant restaurants.

But our last night in Paris was unexpectedly extraordinary. We were taking an evening stroll and sharing a bottle of Chardonnay, which we drank straight from the bottle. Slightly intoxicated, we were looking for a vacant alley where we could indulge Jeff's outdoor sex fantasy.

We couldn't find an empty alleyway, and somehow stumbled upon a large group of people who had gathered at a mini amphitheater along the Seine River. An old man sat on the edge of the river with his radio playing Argentinian accordion music while groups of people seductively danced the tango.

Beautiful Parisian women with off-the-shoulder dresses and wearing flowers in their hair walked up to total strangers and invited them to dance by the water's edge.

It was all so sensual, Jeff and I took a seat, joining other spectators who sat on the stone banks, watching like voyeurs. Mesmerized, we were unable to tear our eyes away from the passionate dancers whose movements reminded us of lovers engaged in sex acts with their clothes on.

Back at the hotel later that night, our pleasure during lovemaking was heightened by having witnessed such uninhibited, sensual dancing.

I could have easily stayed in Paris for another whole week if it weren't for the fact that I was unable to get in touch with Brandon. He hadn't answered any of my calls or texts, and I was eager to get back home and touch base with him.

At the airport, getting through customs took forever and we almost missed our flight. By the time we boarded the plane, I was jittery and on edge.

"Is everything okay with you?" Jeff asked.

"I'm fine," I said with a hint of annoyance.

"Are you sure?" He stroked my hair and gave me one of his trademark smiles as he tried to coax me into a better mood.

"I'm fine, really," I said, manufacturing a tight smile. "The reality of going back to real life is starting to hit me, and I'm a little sad that the honeymoon is over."

"The honeymoon is not over; it's just beginning. We need to talk about our living arrangements, Claire. I want you with me all the time, and I'm starting to feel slightly off-kilter, knowing that after we land, we'll part ways and go to separate houses."

I would have been delighted to talk about planning a future with Jeff at any time except now. All I could focus on was Brandon. I pulled my phone out and called him again. *Pick up, Brandon. Pick up!* My heart thundered when I got his voicemail again. I was so worried about him, I was beginning to feel a tightness in my chest.

I wondered if Ava had said or done something to cause him to withdraw. Was she jealous of the relationship Brandon and I were developing? Had she forbade him from communicating with me?

So many questions swirled in my head. Then, it occurred to me that it was possible Brandon had lost his job. He'd never done well in structured environments and found it nearly impossible to adhere to rules and regulations. I was surprised he'd lasted as long as he had. The poor kid was probably embarrassed to tell me he no longer had a means of income.

Convincing myself that nothing terrible had happened, and that Brandon was merely brooding over losing his job, I was finally able to relax and enjoy Jeff's company.

When Jeff dozed off mid-flight, I was free to power on my phone and bombard Brandon with a string of urgent messages.

"Sorry, ma'am, you can't have your device on at this time," the flight attendant reminded me with a kind smile.

I nodded, shut off my phone, and stuck it in my bag. Then I asked for a blanket and cuddled up next to Jeff and fell into a deep sleep.

The baggage claim area was chaotic, yet Jeff was perfectly calm. He seemed refreshed and serene, the way you're supposed to feel after an amazing vacation. But I was a basket case, pacing, scowling at the carousel of luggage, my body poised to lurch forward and snatch my bags the moment they appeared.

After twenty-five minutes had elapsed, I gestured agitatedly toward the carousel. "For the love of God, why is this taking so long?"

"Things take a bit longer after an international flight. Be patient, love. I'm sure it'll only be a few more minutes." Jeff gave me a flicker of a weary smile and reached for my hand, brushing his fingers against my skin, attempting to soothe me.

But I found the movement of his flesh swishing against mine more annoying than calming, and I slid my hand out of his.

He looked at me in surprise and then thoughtfully stroked his chin. "Something's been bugging you from the moment we boarded the plane in Paris. Wanna talk about it?"

"It's Brandon. He hasn't been taking my calls or responding to my texts, and I'm worried sick."

Jeff scoffed. "*That's* what's bugging you?" He shook his head pityingly. "Claire, you have to get a grip...you've only been gone a week. When I was Brandon's age, I didn't call my mom for weeks at a time."

"You don't understand," I said curtly. "Listen, I can't stick around here any longer. Do me a favor and pick up my luggage, and take it back to your place. I'll stop by and get it tomorrow."

"What're you planning to do?"

I looked in the direction of the windows and spotted a line of waiting cabs. "I'll hop in a cab," I said and turned around and walked briskly toward the exit sign.

"Claire!" Jeff called out.

I whirled around. "I'll call you," I promised and began trotting across the vast room and out the door.

"Where to?" the driver asked.

"Uh...I need to make a quick stop on MacDade Boulevard in Woodlyn."

"What's the address?"

"I don't know the exact address, but the apartment building is a few blocks from the SuperFresh. I'll recognize it when we get there. And, uh...can you wait for me?"

"I can wait, but you have to pay the fare for that trip, and then I have to turn the meter back on."

"No, problem; I understand."

Throughout the thirty-minute trip, I continued to call Brandon. I no longer expected him to pick up, but I kept calling. I couldn't help myself.

We arrived in Woodlyn, and I guided the cabbie to Ava's building. After hastily paying the fare, I hopped out and raced to the entrance. Two unsavory-looking characters were hanging around smoking joints. The smell of marijuana was strong in the air. One guy was Caucasian with stringy brown hair and the other was African American, short and squat with long, reddish-gold-tinted dreadlocks.

"Do you know a woman named Ava who lives in this building?" I asked.

"Ava, who?" asked the black guy.

"Ava Stephenson," I said and when the name didn't seem to register with him, I quickly began to describe her in a breathless rush of words. "She's thin, lots of tattoos, purple-ish, multicolored hair. She drives an old, beat-up Honda.."

Picking up on the desperate ring in my voice, the guy with the dreads squinted at me as if suddenly struck by a brilliant idea. "I might know her," he said challengingly.

"How much?" I asked, cutting to the chase.

"Uh, fifty bucks?" He cut his eyes at his buddy.

"A hundred," the white guy quickly piped in.

Paying for the information wasn't an issue, but I hesitated, fearing the two men would snatch my purse and take off running the moment I began scrounging inside, searching for my wallet.

As if reading my mind, the black guy said, "Yo, lady, we too high to run off with your bag. My legs feeling like noodles right about now." Both men broke into raucous laughter, slapping hands over the absurd idea of them attempting to run.

Nervously, I fingered through the bills in my wallet and extracted two fifties.

"Ava's in apartment two-fifteen," the squat black man informed.

I hurried inside the vestibule area, scanned the numbers on the doorbells and then frantically pressed the button of two-fifteen.

"Yeah?" The voice that came over the intercom was unmistakably Ava's, and my dislike of her was so intense, I involuntarily shuddered at the sound of the single word she'd uttered.

"Is Brandon there? It's Claire—his mother."

"He's not here," she said without a trace of emotion.

"Well, where is he?" I practically shrieked.

"How the hell should I know. I don't keep tabs on him. Dude packed his shit yesterday, and I told him good riddance and peace out! He probably went back home…where else would he go?"

"Thank you," I muttered. Though Ava didn't deserve a polite word from me, I was genuinely grateful to find out that Brandon was safe and sound at home.

I sprinted past the men I'd paid and raced to the cab, and breathlessly gave the driver my home address. "Can you hurry?" I asked in a demanding tone that was unlike me.

"I gotta stay within the speed limit, lady," he responded, refusing to be bullied by me.

Chapter 13

The cab's brakes squealed loudly as it came to a stop in front of my house. The house was pitch-black and I craned my neck and squinted up at Brandon's bedroom window, searching for the dim light of the TV or his computer. But his room was as dark as the rest of the house.

A gnawing worry settled in the pit of my stomach. Where was my child? Was he so forlorn and heartbroken that he was wandering the streets of the city? He couldn't possibly be in Middletown; the police would have escorted him home. In our small town, drifters and loiterers were not tolerated.

After paying the driver, I flung the door open. Under normal circumstances, I'd have used the brick walkway, but being in a rush, I took the quickest route to the front door and dashed across the lawn, uncaringly trampling my lovely flower garden.

Inside, I clicked on lights as I made my way from the living room, through the dining room, and into the kitchen. Everything was as I'd left it. Not a sign that Brandon had been in the house.

Calling his name, I took the stairs two at a time, and when I reached the landing, I knew something was dreadfully wrong. My hand went to my chest as I gawked at Brandon's closed door.

I'd left his bedroom door open when I'd left for Paris. If he was in there, why wasn't he answering me?

"Brandon?" I whispered as I hovered near his door. I tapped softly and when he still didn't answer, my stomach twisted in a tight knot. My hand fisted limply around the knob and I stepped inside the darkened room.

I hesitated briefly before flicking on the light switch. I had to brace myself for a note stating that he'd fled the area in search of himself. I assumed that running off to India or some other foreign land was the kind of thing a hopelessly lost and brokenhearted young man would do.

But Brandon didn't have any real world experience. Or enough money to travel very far. I trembled in fear thinking of the dangerous situations he'd encounter trying to make it on his own in this cold, cruel world.

Bravely, I flicked the switch and in an instant, I found myself down on the floor. I wasn't sure if I'd dropped with a hard thud or had slid down the wall in a slow swoon.

From my position on the floor, I could see the wheels of the swivel chair and Brandon's sneakers. My eyes roamed upward from the ankles of his jeans up to the knees. Then I had to lift my head to figure out why he was sitting so still. Some part of my brain had known when I hit the floor, but I continued observing curiously and saw that his slumped torso was leaning sideways and his mass of curly hair hung to one side. His lifeless eyes were unfocused, staring out at nothing. My eyes landed on the hole in his right temple and lingered briefly on the clumps of blood that clotted his beautiful hair.

When I spotted a gun in his lap that looked vaguely familiar, my brain began to process what had happened. Horrified, my mouth stretched open wider than I would have ever thought possible.

It was a silent scream at first. Next, a sound that was a lot like a siren, emerged from the depths of my soul.

I couldn't recall dialing 9-1-1, but someone had—maybe a neighbor. They found me in a clump on the floor and assuming I was hurt, two people began administering to me. "No, no. I'm okay, but my son needs medical attention. Hurry! Please! He shot himself and I think he's dying."

For some unknown reason, I was placed on a gurney and rushed out of the house. I kept struggling to sit up and check to see if Brandon was okay. Surely my child wasn't dead. My eyes had been playing tricks on me. It was a flesh wound, and the paramedics were going to fix him up and release him from the hospital tonight. Or perhaps they'd keep him overnight for observation.

But why weren't they rushing out of the house with him? Every second counted and I became agitated wondering why they were taking so long. I kept asking for him, and the paramedics exchanged surreptitious glances.

Before they lifted me into the ambulance, I turned my head and saw two other paramedics coming out of my house carrying a gurney that held a black body bag.

"Nooo! No, God, no. Not Brandon. Why? Why? Why?" I tried to hurl myself off the gurney so I could get to my son, but I was strapped down. I became wild and feral, thrashing about and crying out his name.

"You have to calm down, Ms. Wilkins," one of the paramedics advised, but I continued kicking and screaming. Suddenly, I felt the sensation of a sharp prick in my arm and the world became blurry before turning completely dark.

I was heavily sedated when the police officers came to my hospital room to question me. "Do you know where your son might have gotten the gun?"

I shook my head, didn't bother trying to speak because I didn't have the strength to formulate words.

"Was he depressed?"

Once again, I responded by shaking my head. He'd been happier than he'd ever been in his life.

"Did you find a note?"

I shook my head. I wanted to tell them I'd never made it over to Brandon's desk, but the words wouldn't come.

"Any idea why your son would commit suicide?"

Suicide! I grimaced and squeezed my eyes shut. That word had become the vilest in the entire English language.

"We realize you're in shock and the doctor said you've been slightly sedated. Here's my card," said one of the men in blue. "If anything important comes to mind, don't hesitate to give me a call."

Refusing to look at the cops any longer, I turned my head and drifted back to sweet, merciful sleep.

In the morning, I awakened to find Veronica sitting in my room. "Claire, I'm so sorry. Is there anything I can do? Do you want me to call your mother in Indiana?"

Still not ready to talk, I shook my head adamantly. I didn't want to see my bitch of a mother. She'd never liked Brandon and it was possible she'd be secretly delighted that he was gone.

"Claire, you have to pull yourself together. If you don't, Howard is going to handle the funeral arrangements, and I know you don't want that."

No, I didn't want that, and I could feel a solitary tear rolling down my face as I shook my head. I wanted to talk to Veronica. Tell her the horror of finding Brandon like that. But I was incapable of speaking. After screaming for so long and so loudly, there was a horrible burn in the back of my throat. Here at the hospital, bouts of nausea were triggered every time I pictured that bloody hole in Brandon's head, and I was spending many of my waking hours huddled over the toilet, retching my guts out, and putting even more of a strain on my vocal cords.

Through a series of nodding and shaking my head, I conveyed to Veronica that I didn't want a formal funeral. I couldn't bear to see Brandon dressed in a suit and lying in a casket. She became my rock, and also personal bodyguard. I didn't want to see or talk to anyone. I just wanted to be left alone in my misery.

When I was released from the hospital, Jeff stopped by to offer his condolences, but I didn't want to see him, either, and Veronica sent him on his way. I had never gotten around to telling her about our affair, but he filled her in, even telling her about our plans to move in together.

But that wasn't going to happen. Not now. Had I not been frolicking around Paris with him, I would have been home to provide comfort to my son when that despicable girl broke his heart, yet again.

Veronica put together a beautiful memorial service that was held at a church I'd never attended. There were only a handful of people in attendance, mostly coworkers and a few neighbors.

I didn't invite Howard. I believed that both he and Ava had equal blame in Brandon's death. Ava hadn't bothered to extend any condolences, and I was glad that she had the decency to stay away from me.

I had no idea that a gun was in the house until I'd seen it on Brandon's lap, and I'd never forgive Howard for negligently leaving it in the attic years ago when he'd moved out. It was an old gun that had once belonged to an uncle or some other relative. Although the gun had little monetary or sentimental value to Howard, what kind of father mistakenly leaves a gun in a home with a child? Suppose

Brandon had stumbled across it when he was a little kid? Suppose he had accidentally shot himself back when he was only nine or ten? My God, seeing him lifeless and bloody at twenty was bad enough, but I would have not survived seeing him like that while he was young and vulnerable and relying on me to protect him from harm.

I wondered if Howard subconsciously wanted Brandon to find it. Did he hate his son that much?

Hurt and infuriated, I didn't invite him to the service nor would I accept any of his numerous calls or respond to his messages of apology for leaving the gun.

With the help of a tranquilizer, I managed to get through the lengthy eulogy that the pastor delivered without crying out in anguish from the pain that viciously cut through me. It was an unbearable suffering that I wouldn't have wished on my worst enemy.

But not even the strongest dose of Xanax could keep me quietly seated when Howard walked into the church with his elegant family in tow. They were fashionably late, I supposed.

The audacity of him showing up at our son's service, when in life, he'd never given him the time of day. Outraged and half-crazed, I leapt to my feet and raced to the middle of the aisle, screaming obscenities at Howard and swinging punches.

"It was your fucking gun, you bastard. You left a loaded gun in the attic with the rest of your discarded things. You killed him and I hate you!" When my punches weren't landing with sufficient force, I began clawing and kicking him in the shins.

I spat at his wife when she foolishly tried to come to his aid, and God forgive me, I even took a swat at one of his twins.

His wife grabbed the three children and ran out of the sanctuary, while I continued my violent attack on Howard.

I don't know why Howard wasn't better able to defend himself against me. Maybe the sudden attack took him off guard or perhaps it was the incredible strength and stamina that I possessed while momentarily crazed and out of my mind with grief. It took Winking Walter, the pastor, and a custodial employee to get me off of Howard, but I made sure I took a chunk out of his cheek before I was done with him.

Holding his bloody face, he exited the sanctuary firing curses at me and pressing buttons on his phone, calling the police.

I should have felt a modicum of satisfaction, but after I calmed, I was even more devastated that after releasing all that pent-up rage, I still didn't have what I wanted: my son.

"Brandon," I whimpered softly. "Brandon," I cried out a little louder. "Braaaaaaaaandon!" I screamed at the top of my lungs.

Police arrived and after assessing the situation, an ambulance was called. The same paramedics hauled me off to the hospital, but this time I ended up in the psych ward.

Chapter 14

I was retained in the psychiatric wing of Middletown Hospital for thirty days. If I'd had it my way, I would have stayed there forever. Being cut off from society was the perfect escape from reality.

The best part about being a mental patient was the drugs that kept me numb all day, sparing me the heartbreaking emotions that came with the unspeakably tragic loss of my only child. At first the clinical team tried to stick me in group therapy sessions, but since I contributed nothing to the conversations and merely sat there with my mouth agape and with my tongue lolling out the corner of my mouth, I was soon absolved of that therapeutic requirement.

And so I was left alone in my room where I sat staring out the window for hours at a time. Sadly, there was nothing outside the window that elicited even a modicum of interest or joy. Not the sunshine that glinted through the trees and not the parade of visitors, carrying flower arrangements or vibrantly colored balloon bouquets.

More drugs were administered at night, allowing me to sleep for twelve-hour stretches. For the first few blissful moments of awakening, I believed Brandon was still alive, and I'd swing my legs off the bed to go check on him. But when my feet hit the cold tile floor of my hospital room, I realized that something was wrong.

Then unbearable grief would hit me with a tremendous force that sent me crashing to the floor.

In my mind's eyes, as I lay in a crumbled heap, I'd relive the horror, and in my mind's eye, I'd see a macabre montage of that terrible night: the gun on his lap, blood-caked curls, and Brandon's dead eyes.

Too drugged-up and too weak to scream in anguish, I was reduced to whimpering like a wounded animal. Despite my lack of physical strength, I was capable of emitting those mournful sounds unrelentingly throughout the course of an entire day. But I was never left to suffer for too long. One of the nurses always came to my rescue with a magical pill that put me in a zombie-like state and relieved my suffering.

After thirty days, I was released from the hospital with an arsenal of prescriptions. Veronica not only picked me up and drove me home, but she also went through the mail that had been piling up during my hospital stay. Among the correspondence was an envelope so thick it threatened to burst open.

"This is a restraining order from Howard," Veronica said gravely, holding up the document. "It says you have to stay five-hundred yards away from him, his wife, and kids or you'll be arrested."

Having only a vague memory of attacking Howard, I merely nodded in agreement.

She searched through my personal papers and located my insurance policy.

She let out a whistle when she realized the huge amount of money I would receive as the beneficiary. "I always thought there was a clause that denied benefits to suicides."

I flinched.

"I'm sorry, Claire. I won't ever mention that word again."

"Thank you," I whispered, feeling too frail and vulnerable to speak in a normal pitch.

Changing the subject, she waved a manila envelope. "This is the paperwork for your extended leave of absence. All you have to do is sign the places marked 'X' and I'll fill in all the blanks."

"Thanks, Veronica," I murmured softly.

"Don't worry about it, kiddo."

Though anguishing pain was now part of my everyday existence, for some reason, being referred to as "kiddo" at my age, elicited a tiny smile from me.

"It's good to see you smile, Claire," she said, gazing at me and nodding in approval. "But...you're skinny as a skeleton, and that concerns me. I filled up your freezer with frozen meals I picked up from the supermarket. It's all crap; it's terribly unhealthy...loaded with sodium and all kinds of preservatives, but it's better than eating nothing. I'll check on you every couple of days, but in the meantime, please promise that you'll eat."

"I'll eat," I whispered, knowing full well that I wouldn't. I had no interest in food. The most I could get down was a few swallows of water and a couple bites of fruit.

"I'm serious, Claire. I'm getting the feeling you're trying to starve yourself. I'm scared to ask how many pounds you've lost. You look so frail and malnourished, I'm afraid you're going to end up hospitalized and hooked up to a feeding tube if you don't start putting some food in your stomach."

The threat of living with a feeding tube caused something to click, and I concluded that I had two choices: end my miserable existence or make an attempt to start living again.

I chose life because I was too much of a coward to gobble down a handful of pills.

I couldn't expect Veronica to deliver my groceries for the rest of my life and eventually, I set up an account with a nearby grocer and had food delivered. In fact, everything I needed was delivered. I hadn't driven my car since before leaving for Paris, and I kept telling myself to go out to the driveway and check to see if the battery had died. But each time I attempted to leave the house, I would only make it as far as the front door.

I suspected that neighbors wanted a glimpse of the poor woman whose son had taken his life, and for the sake of gossip, they wanted to see how I was holding up. I didn't want to exert the effort to wave a hand at anyone or even flutter my fingers in greeting. I didn't want any interactions.

Unable to bring myself to step outside, I wondered if I suffered from agoraphobia.

When the holiday season rolled around, my mother had the unmitigated gall to call and invite me to spend Thanksgiving with her. This was the same woman who treated my son as if he were an alien simply because he didn't act like other kids his age, running around noisily and chattering nonstop.

When my mother had drunkenly made snide comments about Brandon, I'd never expressed my feelings. Instead, I'd stopped speaking—cut her out of my life without telling her how badly she'd hurt my feelings.

Today, I wouldn't be the wimp I'd been in the past. I was liable to slap my mother senseless if she as much as mentioned Brandon's name. But being charged with yet another assault was bound to land me in jail instead of the psychiatric ward. Therefore, in light of the fact that inflicting bodily harm upon my mother was not an option, it was best that I stayed far, far away from her.

Around mid-December, I received flowers from Jeff with a note that read: *Thinking of you with warm feelings, Jeff.*

He'd sent a Christmassy arrangement of red and white tulips that looked radiant amongst green Douglas fir. The bouquet was decorated with candy canes, frosted pinecones, and tied around the clear glass vase was a red satin ribbon. It was beautiful, and surprisingly, the flowers lifted my spirits, reminding me of the healing nature of plants.

But I still wasn't ready to communicate with Jeff, and doubted if I ever would be. Hopefully, he was living his life and not waiting around for him and me to pick up where we'd left off.

Jeff was a good guy. He'd treated me better than any other man ever had, yet I couldn't continue our relationship. I was an empty shell, unwilling to hold up my end of basic conversation and completely incapable of gaiety or laughter.

I was grieving, goddamnit, and I refused to apologize for it! I wished people would leave me alone and stop waiting for me to finally get on with my life. I had no life without Brandon. Without him, I was merely existing.

What finally drove me out of the house was the desire to be surrounded by greenery. After Jeff's flowers wilted and had to be thrown in the trash, I went through a form of depression that had nothing to do with my grief, and I realized that I needed friends. Not human beings, but green friends. It was a known fact that the benefits of plants went beyond their physical beauty. They also reduced stress and people were generally happier when interior landscaping enhanced their environment.

In addition to an innate yearning to feel better, I also had an overwhelming desire to stick my fingers in soil and begin nurturing something that would thrive under my maintenance and care. I could have easily ordered seeds and bulbs and soil online. But I was so eager to get started, I began throwing on clothes immediately. I sprayed Visine in my eyes that were bloodshot from constant crying. I grabbed my keys and said a little prayer that my car would start.

The motor was sluggish, but when it eventually turned over, I zipped out of the driveway with a sense of excitement I hadn't thought possible. My grief hadn't subsided, not in the least, but I was able to tuck it down deep enough to allow myself to get out of the house and accomplish a task that was important to me.

There was a premier nursery in the city with top quality plants and a vast selection of everything I would need to bring vibrant life into my home. But with the roads being slippery from a recent coating of snow, I thought it best to stay close to my neighborhood. There was a nearby Home Depot that had a fairly decent garden center and a large enough inventory for me to get started on my project.

Pushing a cart inside Home Depot, I whizzed past a series of aisles that displayed lighting, ceiling fans, plumbing equipment, and power tools. I briefly stopped and inspected a row of toilet seats, recalling that there was a small rip in the cushioned seat in the downstairs powder room. Looking for an elongated white, cushioned seat, I found myself humming along with the music that was playing in the store as I surveyed the choices.

Something was happening. The dark cloud of despair was lifting somewhat. Did I dare hope that I might slowly begin to feel like a normal person again?

Standing on my tiptoes, I reached up and rather clumsily pulled a cream-colored seat off the overhead shelf and stumbled backward, accidentally bumping into a shopper behind me. When I turned around to offer an apology, I found myself staring into the face of the last person in the world that I ever wanted to see—Ava! And if the shock of being face-to-face with someone I hated with every fiber of my being wasn't bad enough, the sight of her protruding pregnant belly stole my breath away and nearly knocked me to my knees.

Chapter 15

Equally startled to see me, Ava gave a little gasp, and then tried to hurry away. But I grabbed her, clutching the sleeve of her shiny pink-and-black, animal-print jacket, which clashed badly with her tri-colored, yellow, navy, and pale green hair.

She tried to yank herself out of my grasp, but I held on to the fabric, entwining it inside my fist.

"Why didn't you tell me?" I demanded harshly.

"Why would I bother? You knew the plan, and you made it clear that you weren't happy about us trying to start a family."

"That was before Brandon—" I squeezed my eyes shut and shook my head ruefully, unable to complete the sentence, unable to bring myself to utter the word, *died*. "Clearly, the circumstances have changed dramatically. I can't believe that despite everything that's happened, you didn't have the common decency to let me know. How could you be so heartless?"

She gestured nonchalantly. "I probably would've mentioned it if I hadn't heard about you flipping out. With you being locked up in the, uh, loony bin and all, I didn't think telling you would make any difference."

Mean to the bone and completely unremorseful about the role she'd played in Brandon's decision to take his life, Ava smirked at me. I wanted to strangle her with my bare hands, but lashing out in violence wasn't the answer. She was carrying a part of Brandon inside her and I had to play nice until the baby was born.

But the moment that baby took its first breath, I planned to file for legal custody. Over my dead body would Ava and that girl, Muffy raise my precious grandchild. They both were unsuitable parents who saw nothing wrong with burdening the state with the financial responsibility of the child.

My mind was racing. If I expected my plan to work, I had to pull myself together. Had to get off my meds and return to work. No judge would turn over a newborn to a full-on whack job that was too nuts to function without prescription drugs and unable to hold down a job. In court, I would present as a model citizen, and I planned to hire a pitbull of a lawyer that could win my case even if my mental health was called into question.

Luckily, I had quite a windfall saved. Brandon's college tuition money was still sitting in the bank. And I'd never touched a dime of the support checks Howard had sent over the years. I'd let that money pile up in the bank and had planned on giving it to Brandon when he turned twenty-five. A hefty nest egg like that would have given him a good start into his adult life.

"How many months are you?" I asked, returning my attention to Ava, and loosening my grip on her sleeve at the same time.

"Six," she said dully.

I did the math in my head and deducted that she'd gotten pregnant back in June, probably around the time that she'd told Brandon she was ovulating. Apparently, she'd never admitted to him that they had successfully conceived. The conception had probably been a secret between her and Muffy, and when she no longer required Brandon's services, she'd broken his heart to pieces.

When the police returned Brandon's belongings to me—the clothes he was wearing, the items in his pockets, including his cell phone—it took a few months for me to muster the strength to power on his phone and read the text messages between him and Ava.

From what I ascertained, she'd started an argument with him over a video game he'd purchased with money I'd given him to buy personal items. He was already giving her his entire paycheck, but apparently she resented him spending any amount of money on himself.

It pained me to remember the acrid words she'd hurled at him in those vicious texts. As I stood facing her in the toilet seat aisle of Home Depot, I could have broken down and cried when recalling how he'd begged and pleaded for her to give him one more chance, promising to never withhold money from her again. The saddest thing he'd confided to her was that the way she treated him had made him feel insignificant and life no longer seemed worth living.

She texted him back: *Stop whining like a little bitch and do it already. Oh, that's right, I forgot...you don't have the balls to off yourself.*

Ava had goaded Brandon into suicide. As far as I was concerned, she might as well have put the gun in his hand. Filled with rage, I looked into her hateful face and clenched my teeth so tightly, it was a wonder they didn't crumble inside my mouth.

"So, have you had a sonogram? Do you know whether it's a boy or girl?" I asked in a cheerful tone.

"It's a boy," she said dully.

"Oh, that's wonderful!" I wanted to suggest she name him Brandon, but I didn't want to overstep my boundaries. I planned to change his name to Brandon after I got full custody and had legally adopted him. "Are you taking your prenatal vitamins?" I asked, thinking of the baby's well-being while also marveling over the intensity of my hatred for Ava.

"Yeah, I take 'em," she responded with a hint of irritability, and then looked around distractedly. "Listen, I'm in a rush and I gotta go. It was...um...good to see you, Ms. Wilkins."

"Please, call me Claire." I patted her hand affectionately. "Well, now that we know the gender of my grandchild, I have to go shopping for baby things. I can't wait to set up a nursery at my house. You'll never have to worry about a babysitter, dear." Ugh, I wanted to call her *bitch* instead of *dear*, but I was playing her game of deception. And I was playing to win!

"How are you holding up, moneywise?"

At the mention of money, a glint appeared in her eyes. "I'm doing okay, but the state is only paying for my medical expenses. They won't give me any cash until the baby is here." She patted her stomach. "I'm trying to eat right for my child's sake, but organic food, green juice, and the rest of that healthy stuff costs more than I can afford." Suddenly chatty, Ava poured it on. "The doctor might put me on bedrest soon, and if that happens I'm going to need a lot of help."

"What's going on that you'd need to be on bedrest?" I asked, my concern heightening.

"I miscarried when I was nineteen and I'm considered a high risk." She shrugged like it was no big deal.

Nervous about her ability to reach full term without miscarrying, I had an unpleasant image of me having to haul groceries to her apartment once a week while she was on bedrest—groceries that she and Muffy would devour while cuddled together watching TV.

As if reading my mind, Ava said, "Muffy walked out on me and took the car, so now I have to get around on public transportation, which sucks." Playing on my sympathy, she slyly glanced downward.

"Do you need a ride home?" I didn't want her walking to the bus stop and possibly slipping on ice and hurting my grandson.

"No, I have a ride waiting for me in the parking lot."

"Well, I want to help out in any way I can, so please don't hesitate to call me," I said, knowing what a greedy little money grubber she was.

"I don't have your number, Claire."

Now that the topic of money had come up, Ava didn't seem to be in as big of a rush. With a smirking smile, and giving me the impression that a money-counting machine was going off in her head, she took out her phone and patiently waited for me to rattle off my number.

After I gave her my number, she took off, disappearing into the crowd of holiday shoppers.

Excited about the baby news, I stood in place for a few moments, smiling and hugging myself. Then I flung the toilet seat I'd been holding back on the shelf.

No longer interested in toilet seats or in the garden center, I abandoned my shopping cart and exited the store. I had a new lease on life, and I preferred to make plans to nurture a living and breathing human being instead of a family of houseplants.

The blood of my blood—my son's child! I was getting an opportunity for a do-over, and I vowed that this time I would get it right. My grandson was not going to grow up to be socially awkward or become a recluse. I would make sure he began interacting with other kids at an early age, and I envisioned myself setting him up with playdates shortly after he learned how to walk.

I'd failed to protect Brandon from an uncaring, narcissistic sperm donor who denied him love and destroyed his self-esteem. But I wouldn't fail this child. He was going to feel loved and cherished the moment he exited his birth mother's womb and was cradled in my arms. I wouldn't allow anyone to psychologically damage him—neither Howard nor Ava would get the opportunity to mess with his head.

In the parking lot, I checked online for the nearest Babies"R"Us. I couldn't wait to get my hands on cute little hooded pajamas , soft booties and beanies, and tiny jeans!

Before backing out of my parking spot, I checked my rearview mirror and had to slam on the brakes when a car whizzed past me from behind. I noticed the driver, an older man, had an angry expression. He looked familiar, but I couldn't place him. Even more strange, seated next to him was none other than Ava. Judging by her frenetic hand gestures, the two of them were in the midst of an argument.

I racked my brain for a full ten minutes, trying to remember how I knew the guy. Then it finally dawned on me that the driver was Winking Walter, the man who volunteered twice a week in my department at the zoo.

What in the world was he doing with Ava? Were they related— was he an uncle or a grandparent? Or was something else going on? As unscrupulous as Ava was, I wouldn't put it past her to scam a senior citizen out of his retirement fund.

Worried for Walter, I considered calling Veronica to find out if he had a young, rough-at-the-edges relative living in our area. I dug my phone out of my purse and then dropped it back inside. If I contacted Veronica, I'd have to reveal the nature of my association with Ava, and that was something I wasn't ready to divulge.

Chapter 16

Although I didn't correct the technician at the ultrasound imaging center when she referred to me as Ava's "mom," my body tensed in protest. But my discomfort subsided as soon as the show began! The joy of seeing live footage of my unborn grandson tossing and turning and even smiling in 3D was an exciting adventure. The high-quality, detailed image of the baby that I was given as a keepsake was worth every second of the discomfort I experienced having to spend time with Ava.

The baby looked so much like Brandon, my heart swelled with love. I couldn't wait to drop Ava off at her place, get back home, and stare at the picture in private.

But I should have known that an opportunist like Ava would expect to be rewarded for enduring a second ultrasound at my request. After we left the imaging center, she complained that her boobs had gotten so big they were bursting out of all her maternity bras.

The trip to the mall to get her larger-sized bras turned into a full-fledged shopping spree for Ava. She managed to wheedle not only maternity bras out of me but also a ridiculously expensive pair of Nikes, a fluffy coat with a fur-trimmed hood, cosmetics from Macy's, a shopping cart full of toiletries from CVS, and several cases of Snapple iced tea, which she ignorantly claimed was a healthy substitute for the beer she'd given up during the pregnancy.

I didn't even bother to try and educate her about the high sugar content in iced tea and the harmful effect that sugar had on a fetus. My precious little grandson only had a few more months to be subjected to Ava's sugar cravings.

Unbelievably, after I loaded up my trunk with her shopping bags, Ava announced that she was dying for a Chai Latte from Starbucks.

Spending an entire day with someone I loathed was so unpleasant and exhausting, I had the sensation of lightheadedness as I sat across from her in Starbucks.

She didn't simply get the Chai Latte, but had greedily ordered practically everything on the menu. There was a feast before her: an Ancho Chipotle Chicken sandwich, Hearty Veggie and Brown Rice Salad Bowl, Apple Fritter, and two orders of Butterfly Cookies along with the Chai Latte. There was no way she could consume all that food, but it was as if she were compelled to get as much out of me as she possibly could.

As she prattled on and on about the difficulty of the pregnancy—stretch marks, insomnia, heartburn—I escaped her never-ending complaints by daydreaming about the future child prodigy I would be raising. A concert pianist, a math whiz, or maybe a software developer, fluent in dozens of programming languages.

"So, what do you think? Can we start looking into cosmetic surgeons next week?" Ava asked, cutting into my thoughts.

"Hmm?" I had no idea what she was talking about.

"I heard it was best to get consultations with at least four doctors before selecting one."

"I'm sorry, I have no idea what you're talking about," I said, sincerely baffled though I strongly suspected she was about to hit me up for more money.

"I told you that after the baby comes, I want a tummy tuck. And I'm going to have to do something about these stretch marks, so we need to start setting up appointments with qualified surgeons."

We? I almost laughed in her face. She was a bigger fool than she thought *I* was if she truly believed that I was going to be an unlimited source of revenue for her for the next eighteen years. But she was too narcissistic to realize that I'd have no more use for her after my grandson was safely in my arms.

But needing her to remain happy and healthy until the baby arrived, I pretended to go along with the farce. "Sure, we can look into that, but what's the rush? You have to wait a couple of months after giving birth before it's safe to have surgery," I said, sounding wise and giving the impression that I gave a damn about her body image issues.

"So, have you thought about names?" I asked, knowing full well that I was going to name him Brandon.

"Not really." She turned up a corner of her lip as if she couldn't be so bothered as to stress her brain with such an insignificant topic. She had better things to think about—like improving her body, for instance. And how to bilk the welfare system.

She was a despicable girl, not fit to be a mother, and the more she revealed her repugnant character, the better I felt about duping her into believing that I gave a damn about her.

Her phone jangled and she frowned at the screen for a few moments before deciding to take the call.

"What do you want, Walter?" she asked, wearing her trademark sour expression. "No, I don't think so," she muttered dismally. "Maybe tomorrow." There was a lengthy pause, followed with, "I'm not sure."

My interest was piqued at the mention of Walter's name, and I was more than curious to learn the nature of their relationship. But hearing only Ava's end of the conversation didn't provide any answers.

After she hung up, I manufactured a hopeful expression, and asked with widened eyes, "New boyfriend?"

Swallowing my pride, I pretended that I found it utterly charming that she'd managed to move on with her love life so soon after the tragic death of my son.

"No, he's more like an associate."

"Oh?" I leaned forward, encouraging her to continue, but Ava pressed her lips together, literally shutting down.

"I don't see any harm in your moving on," I said reassuringly, coaxing her to open up. "You're young and life goes on...right?"

She grimaced. "Ew. It's not like that. Walter's old enough to be my grandfather. He's just a lonely old man." She chuckled sardonically. "He doesn't have any family and neither do I, so I suppose you can say he sort of adopted me. But he can be a nuisance, always checking on me. You know what I mean?"

I nodded, but I had no idea what she meant. I wanted to bombard her with questions. When and where did she meet him? Did he help her out with finances? Was she aware that he had a lady friend who kept him pretty occupied with salsa dancing and long hikes? Veronica even joined him in bird watching, so there was no reason for Walter to be lonely. Did he secretly enjoy the company of a younger woman— albeit a hardened, street-tough, and pregnant one. Was he Ava's sugar daddy? Actually, sugar granddaddy was more accurate.

The way Ava had been greedily squeezing me for money from the moment I'd shown an interest in her pregnancy proved the kind of mercenary person she was. I couldn't imagine her spending time with an old man or anyone else without expecting compensation. That was simply the way she was wired.

I wondered if I should speak to Veronica and find out what she knew about her boyfriend's relationship with Brandon's "baby mama." Ugh. I hated that expression, but it fit Ava perfectly.

I thought about it and decided to mind my own business. Troubling Veronica with my suspicions could possible backfire. The less she or anyone else knew about my scheme to obtain custody of Brandon's child, the easier it would be to pull it off.

Ava's phone pinged incessantly as she and someone—Walter, maybe—texted back and forth. Ava was a sneaky one. She seemed to always be up to something. I hoped she wasn't scamming Walter out of his retirement money. But if that was the case, then it was his own fault for being a dirty old man.

We finished our lattes in silence and then I drove Ava home. I helped lug the numerous items I'd purchased for her to the elevator and then trudged back to the car and returned carrying the heavy cases of iced tea. After all I'd done for her during the course of the day, she had the nerve to ask if I'd be available to take her to get her hair trimmed tomorrow.

I had to count to ten before solemnly nodding.

Of course, she didn't merely want me to provide transportation. She'd expect me to foot the bill, and afterward she'd think of something else she desperately needed. The girl was a bottomless pit of need and yearning. It was absolutely sickening the way she was never satisfied. My heart hurt for Brandon. He was so in over his head with Ava. He didn't have the cunning or savvy to handle a calculating little viper like her.

Snow flurries slowed down my drive home, and when I finally made it through the front door, I took off my coat, scarf and boots, and curled up on the couch. I pulled out the ultrasound image and stared at it until tears of joy filled my eyes. The baby was the splitting image of Brandon with a head full of dark curls and a keen nose that turned up slightly at the tip. And his estimated fetal weight was already four pounds. My grandson was going to be a big, beautiful, healthy boy!

Being blessed with a second chance to be a good mother was oh so worth the expense of indulging Ava's whims and enduring the distastefulness of being in her presence.

Not once had she apologized for treating my son so cruelly. In fact, she rarely mentioned Brandon's name. Ava was too self-absorbed to be concerned about anyone other than herself. She would be the absolute worst mother in the world, and I'd die before I allowed her to destroy my grandchild's life.

The ultrasound image was proof of life, and it gave me a sense of empowerment. It emboldened me. Feeling brave, I rose from the couch and headed up the stairs as if being pulled by a magnet. Standing outside Brandon's bedroom door, I took a deep breath and opened the door. It was the first time I'd been in his room since that night. I sat at the desk where he'd taken his life. Ran my hands over the roughened surface of the wood.

Tears trickled from my eyes. *Oh, Brandon. I let you down. I didn't protect you from your father. The way he avoided and ostracized you was malicious and you were made to feel that you weren't good enough at an early age. I should have divorced him when you were a toddler, but I stayed—trying to keep up the image of a happy family while hoping that over time, he'd become more accepting of you. But he never changed and by the time our marriage ended, the damage to your psyche had already been done.*

I should have protected you from Ava as well. I knew from the start that she was poison, yet I pushed you into her spider's web when I insisted that you conform to normal behavior...go to school or get a job. You weren't capable. You were too tormented and damaged to fit in with society's norms. And as a mother, I should have known that and I should have accepted you for who you were. Believe me, if I could turn back time, I would. And you'd be right here in your room playing video games. Oh, sweetie, this house is so quiet now. You have no idea how I yearn for the computerized sounds that used to emanate from your room.

But I promise you, I'm going to take good care of your son. I won't stand by helplessly while Ava uses him to get a welfare check. I won't condone her passing on her warped sense of what's normal on to my innocent grandson.

Chapter 17

M y appointment with a family court attorney was very disappointing. According to him, it would have been extremely difficult for me to get custody of the baby without proof that Ava was unfit and/or had endangered the fetus during pregnancy. It didn't matter that Ava had no intention of bettering herself by furthering her education or getting some sort of job training. That she felt deprived to be receiving only medical benefits from the state and was looking forward to receiving a welfare check and food stamps had no bearing on her parenting skills.

"What do you mean by 'endangered the fetus'?" I asked.

"Does she use drugs?"

"I don't think so. I'm pretty certain she drank a lot of beer and smoked a lot of weed before she got pregnant, but I believe she stopped."

"Well, the only way you're going to legally get that baby is if the mother is prosecuted for assault for the illegal use of a narcotic drug while pregnant. And the only way to make that determination is if the infant is harmed or addicted to whatever drug she's using."

Merely imagining a child being brought into this world already addicted to a substance put a severe frown on my face. "The baby's healthy," I said with assurance. "The mother recently had an ultrasound and everything is fine. The problem is, she's narcissistic and she'll damage him emotionally. She's not fit to raise a child."

"That's your opinion, but it won't stand up in a court of law." Growing impatient with me, the lawyer looked at his watch, letting me know the free consultation was over. "If you retain me as your lawyer, we can start building a case against her."

"How long will it take...to uh, build a case?"

He furrowed his brows. "It depends on the evidence being documented. It could take weeks, months...or years."

"Years! You can't be serious. That child won't stand a chance in life if I don't get him away from his mother as soon as possible."

"That may be true, but you have to stay within the bounds of the law. You can't expect a judge to separate a child from his mother because she's not the greatest person in the world."

I snorted. "She's the *worst* person in the world. Do you realize this woman is so toxic, my son committed suicide?"

The lawyer winced and then gazed at me pityingly. "I think there's something else going on. You're grief-stricken, you're angry, and you want to lash out at someone."

"Oh, you're not only an attorney, but you're also a psychologist?" I asked snidely. I stood up, thanked him for his time, and marched out of his office.

I didn't need a lawyer, I decided, and while driving home from his office, I came up with a plan. I would take little Brandon straight from the hospital. By force, if necessary.

With all the money I had saved, including the hefty payout from Brandon's insurance policy, I was pretty well off. Selling my house would bring in another $800,000 or more. I had more than enough to charter a plan to France, a country that was steeped in culture and history. And also a country not likely to extradite me back to the United States for kidnapping.

There was nothing to hold me here. The baby and I would thrive in Paris where citizens enjoyed life with an open attitude. But I would have rules of conduct. I wouldn't allow him to drink coffee and wine like other French children. I would never be that permissive.

I had picked up a little French when Jeff and I visited Paris, but now I'd have to get serious about learning the language.

Thinking about Jeff and Paris saddened me. We'd had something really special, but I now realized we were doomed from the start.

I needed to establish a routine and a pattern of behavior that wouldn't make anyone suspicious about my intention to leave the country with the baby. Going back to work would be the perfect way to establish a routine, and so I called Human Resources and informed them that I'd be returning to work on January fifteenth.

My return to the workplace was awkward to say the least. While I was out on leave, Meghan had been holding down the fort as the acting Director of Horticulture, and when I entered the premises, it was rather unsettling to see her seated at my desk, leisurely twirling around in my chair, laughing into the phone as she made plans to go out for drinks after work.

Even more disconcerting, I caught Veronica, whom I'd honestly viewed as a doting mother figure, dutifully placing a piping hot mug of coffee on the desk in front of Meghan. I supposed Veronica's loyalties lie with whoever was in charge of our department.

"Hold on a minute," Meghan said to the person on the phone. Frowning, she looked at me and said, "We weren't expecting you. What're you doing here?"

Meghan's eyes flitted toward Dwight as if he had the answer. He made a face, shrugged his shoulders, and then skulked over to the coffee pot.

"Would you like some coffee, Claire?" Veronica asked guiltily.

When I shook my head, she studied me worriedly as if she feared I might reenact my performance at Brandon's memorial service.

I was waiting for Meghan to get out of my chair and scurry out of the building to attend one of the many committee meetings that she was always running off to in the course of the work day, but when she returned to her phone conversation, it was clear she had no intention of moving.

That's when I noticed the cluster of framed photos of her posing with family and friends. There was even a picture of her cat strategically placed in the center of two potted cacti.

I couldn't have cared less about losing my position to Meghan, but I wondered if I should've pretended to be offended. As I pondered the dilemma, I noticed that everyone was waiting for my reaction. They'd all been at the memorial service and having witnessed my meltdown, they looked concerned that there might be a repeat performance.

Meghan, on the other hand, seemed unfazed. She picked up her phone and returned to the dilemma of where to go for Happy Hour.

I noticed Dwight motioning, trying to get Meghan's attention. "Uh, Meghan?"

"What is it, Dwight?"

"Can I speak to you out in the corridor?"

Meghan told whoever she was talking to that she'd call them back. Begrudgingly, she followed Dwight out into the hallway. The younger members of my team trailed behind Meghan, eager to hear what Dwight had to say.

Veronica and I locked eyes. "They think you're..." She gestured with her finger going in a circle on the side of her head.

"They think I'm crazy?" I asked, embarrassed for myself.

"But that's a good thing. They don't want to provoke you so they'll be on their best behavior," Veronica said, laughing.

My team came back inside and Meghan began clearing her belongings off the desk. "I'll clear out the drawers during my lunch break," she offered, looking apologetic.

I wondered what Dwight had said to her. Knowing his personality, he'd probably said something like, "If you don't want that bitch to go postal on all of us, you better get out of her chair and let her have her desk back."

My team cleared out and Veronica remained. I went through the drawers and discovered piles of mail that dated back at least two months.

"What in the world has Meghan been doing while I was gone?" I asked Veronica.

"As the kids say, she's been chillin'," Veronica replied with a chuckle. Then, taking on a serious expression, she searched my face. "Welcome back, Claire. It's good to see you, but are you sure it's a good idea to come back so soon?"

"Too many memories of Brandon in the house. It's so lonely without him."

"I know, I know," she said soothingly.

"I would have to resume my normal life eventually, and I can't think of a better time than now, when it's not as busy here as it'll get in the spring."

She nodded in understanding and gave my shoulder a squeeze before ambling off to the greenhouse.

There weren't many visitors at the zoo in the middle of January, but we were still responsible for keeping up the appearance of the grounds and the upkeep of the plant life inside the habitats of the animals that were featured in fully enclosed exhibits. And Zoo-Doo was a year-round project.

I immersed myself in the stacks of correspondence before me and when I came up for air, it was already eleven o'clock, which was the time I was supposed to pick up Ava and take her to a consultation with one of the surgeons on her list.

It gave me great pleasure to call her and tell her she had to cancel the appointment.

"Why? I'm dressed and ready to go." She sounded deeply offended.

"There was something at work that needed my attention. I was given the choice of dealing with my responsibilities here at the job or relinquishing my position. It doesn't matter that I'm still grieving, I had to pull myself together and continue to earn a living."

"For fuck's sake, couldn't you have called earlier, like, before I got dressed? It isn't easy getting myself together with a big stomach slowing me down," Ava said in a reprimanding tone.

"Listen, I'm sorry, Ava. But things are so hectic here at work, your appointment completely slipped my mind."

She sucked her teeth.

It didn't matter that I told her my job was at stake and she didn't give a damn about my unremitting grief. It was all about Ava. The girl was unable to empathize. My work schedule was an inconvenience and interfered with my availability to chauffeur her all over town.

"Why don't you call the doctor's office and reschedule your appointments? I'll be available on weeknights after five."

"Evening appointments are not that easy to get," she said testily.

Oh, well! "Then ask for a Saturday appointment."

She let out a groan. "Saturdays are harder to get than weeknights."

Aw, isn't that a shame. "I don't know what to tell you, Ava. I'm bogged down with work right now. You're a resourceful girl; I'm sure you'll think of something," I replied impatiently while wearing a wicked smile.

She uttered a sound of discontent. "I hate to have to call my gentleman friend for transportation. That old buzzard really creeps me out, but I have to put up with him now that you don't have time for me."

She was laying the accusations on really thick, and I didn't want to alienate her. "I apologize, and I'll make sure I'm available for your evening appointments, okay?"

"If you say so," she muttered sullenly. "I'll call you back tomorrow."

She was so full of herself that she really believed I was willing to pay for her cosmetic surgery. What a laugh! The baby and I would be long gone by the time she was cleared to go under the knife. And knowing Ava, she'd probably be more upset over not getting a tummy tuck than she'd be over the loss of her child.

It boggled my mind why someone as selfish as Ava would even consider bringing a child into the world.

A few minutes after getting off the call with Ava, my desk phone rang. It was Shannon Teal from the volunteer department, calling to inform me that Walter Caulfield had resigned from his position in the horticulture department.

I was surprised to say the least. "Did he give a reason?" I asked Shannon.

"No, he just apologized for the short notice."

I thanked her and after hanging up the phone, I drifted into deep thought. It couldn't be a coincidence that Walter had quit on the same day I'd returned. For some reason, he was avoiding me and I was certain that Ava was the reason.

What exactly was going on with those two? And what did he know about my relationship with her? Did he know she was carrying my grandson? There was no point in trying to get any answers from Ava. She was tight-lipped and mysterious when it came to her odd association with Walter.

I should have been grateful that Walter had spared me the awkwardness of having to witness him pretending to be a harmless senior citizen when he was really a lecherous old goat. I didn't have proof, but I strongly suspected that he had the hots for Ava. And I wouldn't put it past her to lead him on.

There was no other explanation for a sixty-something-year-old man hanging around a girl who was forty years his junior. I thought about the argument they were having in the car that day in Home Depot's parking lot. What was that about—a lover's spat?

It was time to have a talk with Veronica. I threw on my coat and braved the frigid cold. I pulled my collar up around my neck as I trekked across the grounds on my way to the greenhouse.

Chapter 18

Inside the greenhouse, a radio played '60s soul music as Veronica puttered around, spritzing plants, clipping browned edges of leaves and talking to them in loving tones as if she were speaking to her own grandchildren, whom she adored.

Hearing the door open and close, she glanced in my direction. "What brings you to my neck of the woods, Claire?" she asked jokingly.

I got right to the point. "How're things with you and Walter?"

"Good. Why do you ask?"

"I thought maybe you two had a little tiff or something."

She gave me a baffled look. "No, we get along just fine. You're hinting around at something...what's going on?"

"Well, Shannon Teal called a few minutes ago and told me that Walter quit his volunteer position."

"He did what?" Veronica set down the plastic spritz bottle and placed an indignant hand on her hip.

"He quit and he didn't offer any explanation. I wondered if he'd mentioned anything to you. Was he unhappy here? Did someone on our team do or say anything to upset him? I honestly thought he enjoyed working with plants, and I thought he was especially fond of working here in the greenhouse with you."

"Well, I thought so, too." She shook her head in utter bewilderment. "There's only one way to get to the bottom of this." She dug her phone out of one of the pockets of her smock and tapped the screen. "It's ringing, but he's not picking up. Now, that's not like Walter at all."

I listened as she left a message, instructing him to call her right away. She perched herself on top of a stool and leaned over, clenching her chin thoughtfully.

"How well do you know him?"

"What're you getting at? As you already know, Walter and I have been dating for months, and I know the man well enough to share my bed with him a couple nights a week. Furthermore—"

I waved my hand, cutting her off. "Whoa! That's too much information."

"Well, you asked," she reminded me sassily.

"Veronica," I said gently. "I think Walter's been leading a sort of double life."

She scowled at me, leaned back, and folded her arms. "Go ahead. Spill the beans."

She was trying to act tough, but it was only an act. I could see hurt creeping in her eyes. She'd been a widow for over fifteen years, and had given up on finding a man as good as her husband. I was sure she wouldn't have gone as far as remarrying, at her age, but she was content with Walter and enjoyed having a companion to share her interests.

"I hate being the bearer of bad news, but I've seen Walter in the company of a young woman...a *really* young woman," I said, stressing the word "really."

"How young?" Her features softened and she appeared to be less concerned.

"Her early twenties."

Veronica let out a guffaw. "You had me worried there for a moment.

He's not leading a double life, Claire. Walter does work for a charitable organization that helps out young women who're in distress over an unplanned pregnancy. These girls don't have families and lack any type of support networks during their pregnancies."

I furrowed my brows. Ava's pregnancy wasn't unplanned. She'd pressured Brandon into impregnating her and brainwashed him into believing he was ready for fatherhood. But I couldn't share that information with Veronica.

"Personally, I'm pro-choice," she continued. "But Walter believes in the right to life. He's pretty passionate about the topic and considers abortions as murder. He admires these girls for choosing adoption over abortion."

Adoption! I gasped inside but outwardly maintained my composure.

"The way I see it, everyone's entitled to their opinion. I steer clear of debates about politics, religion, and I don't get into any discussions about abortions with Walter. When he talks about his work with young girls, I tell him I admire his conviction. He doesn't make a dime nor does he get compensated for the gas he burns carting those girls to their doctors' appointments and driving them around to run errands. He's a good man, Claire. That's why he's in my life. Give me some credit for knowing how to pick 'em." She laughed. "At my age, I think I know a scoundrel when I see one."

"Don't you think it's a little odd that he didn't give you a heads-up about leaving our department? It's so sudden."

Veronica waved a hand dismissively. "Oh, Walter probably got himself a new case. Possibly a girl who's on the fence about putting her child up for adoption. With situations like that, he'll put in extra time, coddling the girl and pretty much holding her hands until the time she gives birth. Usually, the adoptive couple has already been selected and they're devastated when a young woman changes her mind. The organization starts providing financial support for the young woman's basic needs...like paying her rent, providing groceries, and paying for her prenatal care, pretty much at the very beginning of the pregnancy. That said, even though I'm pro-choice, I also have a lot of respect for the idea of valuing life and helping out couples who can't have a child of their own."

Veronica paused and my mind began racing. What the hell kind of a scam was Ava involved in? It figured that a con artist like her was trying to get money from every available source. It seemed criminal that she was deceiving that organization for her own personal gain. Ava was a menace to society and she needed to be locked up. What a poor excuse of a human being!

I'd misjudged Walter. He was actually being victimized and deceived by Ava—just like Brandon had been and probably the lesbian, Muffy as well. Good for Muffy, whoever she was, for having the sense to get away from Ava before she'd depleted her emotionally and financially.

Somehow I got through my first day back at work. I attended a management meeting and noticed that people seemed uncomfortable around me. They didn't know what to say to me. I'd lost count of how many people had muttered, "Sorry for your loss," and then scurried away as if I had a contagious disease.

Maybe if Brandon had been sick or died in a car accident, they'd have the perfect words prepared. *"The Lord always takes the good ones home early."*

But a suicide was a different matter altogether. According to most people's belief system, my son was burning in Hell.

It was fine with me that people were avoiding me. It gave me the opportunity to be alone with my thoughts as I tried to wrap my head around what Ava was up to.

Was she working both the adoption agency and me? It was entirely possible that she was pretending that she wanted me in my grandson's life while knowing full well she intended to give him up for adoption.

If Ava was considering adoption, you could bet it wasn't because she wanted what was best for the child. Most likely there was money involved. In these modern times, couples had to spend big bucks to adopt a child. A chill ran up my spine at the thought of arriving at the hospital only to discover that she'd signed the baby over to adoptive parents.

But didn't I have any legal rights? Couldn't I get an injunction of some type to stop any plans for adoption? If Brandon were alive, Ava certainly couldn't give their child away on a whim. She'd need Brandon's signature. As the baby's paternal grandmother, couldn't I stand in proxy for Brandon and halt what was essentially a criminal act?

Maybe I was letting my imagination run wild, but by the end of the day, there were a million terrifying thoughts running through my head. What would I do if Ava outwitted me and gave the baby away before I had a chance to flee to France with him? I was already attached to my grandson and loved him ferociously. It would kill me to lose him. I couldn't survive the loss of another child.

After work, I swung by Ava's apartment, bearing gifts: a steaming hot Chai Latte and the food items she liked from Starbucks. I'd never been inside her apartment. I'd only gotten as far as the dreary lobby, but needing to keep close tabs on her, I had high hopes that she'd buzz me up.

The buzzer was dirty and germ-ridden. With a gloved finger, I pressed it.

"Yeah?" Ava's voice came over the intercom sounding gruff and pissed off, as usual. She had a bad attitude without having any idea of who was ringing her bell. How could someone who felt such hatred for the world in general find it in her heart to treat a helpless baby with kindness? Ava struck me as the type who'd smack an infant for crying.

"Hi, Ava. It's Claire." The forced perkiness in my tone was so fake, my pitch climbed several notches.

"What do you want?" she asked in a monotone.

"Oh, I just stopped by to drop off a little treat for you. You're eating for two after all. I brought that sandwich you like from Starbucks... the Ancho Chipotle Chicken. And I got you a Chai Latte and some bakery goods."

"Cool. I'll be down in a minute." There wasn't a trace of surprise or joy in her tone, and I certainly didn't detect even a hint of gratitude.

When she came down to the lobby, I noticed that her hair was no longer multicolored, but was now a single, hideous shade of mint green. She was wearing sweat pants and a top that was so snug around her belly, it revealed the imprint of her navel. She looked like she was ready to pop that baby at any moment. On her feet were UGG bedroom slippers that looked brand-new. A gift from Walter to keep her pacified? But why would a good Samaritan work so hard to keep a pregnant girl content? Something was fishy. There had to be more to the story than Walter had told Veronica.

Ava shuffled toward me, scowling. It was obvious she wasn't thrilled to see me. Her sour expression remained in place, even as she removed the bags of goodies from my hands.

What had Brandon seen in her? I wondered for the hundredth time. Maybe there was a comforting sense of familiarity in being with someone with a disposition more miserable than his own.

"How was your consultation?" I asked, trying to elicit a smile from her. I hadn't come over to piss her off. I needed to remain in her good graces until she gave birth.

"The consultation was okay, but I'm not using that doctor. I'm gonna keep looking until I find one that'll fix me up right after I push this baby out."

I sighed. "Ava, that's how they do it in Hollywood. But no reputable doctor in the real world would agree to something so risky."

"What do you care?" she barked, her face contorted in anger. "You're only interested in the baby...not me. So let's keep it real." She jutted out her chin in a way that challenged me to deny her accusation.

My eyes darted downward. "That's not true. I'm very fond of you, Ava." I gave an uncomfortable chuckle that betrayed my sincerity, and so I pressed onward. "How could I not care about the mother of my grandchild. In fact, I'm deeply concerned about your well-being," I added, laying it on thick as I lied through my teeth.

"Well, you should be careful not to get too attached," she said cryptically.

My eyes shot upward in alarm. "What do you mean?"

She paused long enough to make me squirm and it was evident by the glint in her eyes that she enjoyed making me squirm.

"I have to relocate," she blurted.

I waited for her to say more, but she didn't elaborate. Instead she rustled through the Starbucks bags. She pulled out a cookie and began munching on it.

I swallowed hard. "Where and why are you relocating?" I asked anxiously.

"I'm not sure where I'm going, but I have someone helping me find a new place. Anyways..." Her voice trailed off as she took another bite out of the cookie.

I stood there, impatiently waiting for her to finish chewing the damn cookie, but she took yet another bite, informing me that she refused to say another word until she was done eating every damned cookie in the bag.

Livid, I wanted to slap the Starbucks bags out of her hand. God, how I despised Ava. It gave me immense pleasure to imagine grinding the heel of my boot into her face, and pulverizing her features into an unrecognizable bloody mass.

She finished the cookies and then licked crumbs from her finger. "Mmm. Butterfly Cookies are the bomb."

I blinked rapidly as I tried to control my impulse to do her bodily harm. "Ava, it's ludicrous for you to consider moving when you're this late in your pregnancy."

"I don't have a choice. I can't afford the rent anymore."

I looked around at the bleak environment. The rent couldn't have been very high. And according to Veronica, the charitable organization took care of the living expenses of the girls who didn't have sufficient income.

"Why can't you afford to pay the rent? This place seems...well, I'm not deliberately making a dig, but this building appears to be low-income housing."

"Yeah, well, I'm a few months behind."

"What happened?"

"For starters, I used to have two roommates, but they both bailed on me."

My mouth literally fell open. She was accusing Brandon of *bailing* on her? Unable to control my emotions any longer, my facial muscles began to spasm out of control. Anyone looking at me would have thought I was in the midst of a stroke the way one corner of my mouth twitched, an eyebrow shot upward and remained there, and my nostrils flared.

"You're a truly callous and coldhearted girl. How could you say something so insensitive? Brandon took his life because nothing he did for you was good enough."

She sucked her teeth and rolled her eyes. "I knew you blamed me and were only sucking up to me so you could be close to the baby."

"Well, who else would I blame? My son was going above and beyond for you. Putting up with your lesbian relationship and turning over his entire paycheck to you. But nothing satisfied you... and he was a fragile person. He couldn't deal with your verbal abuse."

"Is that what he told you—that I verbally abused him?" Her sneering tone along with the smirk on her face took me over the edge and stinging tears welled in my eyes. "What happened to you in life that made you so heartless? My son is dead because of you. Don't you understand that?"

She scoffed. "If that's what you need to believe to get to sleep at night, then go ahead and place all the blame on me. But in your heart, you know that your son was already fucked up when I met him."

Her words cut so deeply, my hand went up to my heart as if to try and staunch the bleeding.

"I read the texts between you two," I said, continuing to provide evidence that she had pushed Brandon beyond his limit. "He trusted you enough to bare his soul to you and you violated that trust by throwing everything he'd shared with you back in his face. You made him feel worse about himself than he did before he met you."

"Oh, really? Did I make him feel worse than you and his dad made him feel?" she asked smugly.

"*Me* and his dad? I didn't do anything to Brandon except love him."

I was aware of the baseless accusations that Brandon threw in my face whenever he got upset with me, but I couldn't begin to imagine what he really thought of me.

There was no way he remembered the weak person I was while married to his father. Brandon could barely talk back when I stood by helplessly while his father spoke of him harshly. Thoughts whirled in my head, and I briefly went back in time.

"Claire! Come get this kid," Howard barked from his study. Brandon had learned how to open the door and would periodically toddle into his father's private space.

I always rushed to get him as quickly as possible, but Howard would be livid. "Christ, can't you control this idiot kid. I'm trying to get some work done in here!"

Apologetically, I'd scoop up our son. "You can't bother Daddy when he's working," I'd say soothingly, kissing Brandon on the cheek as I closed the door to Howard's study.

I should have kneed my ex in the balls for calling my baby an idiot. But I was so meek back then. Trying to keep the peace. Trying to keep us together as family. My priorities were out of line.

Returning to the present, I glanced at Ava and held her gaze. "What did Brandon say about me?" I asked, feeling so humiliated, my words came out in a trembling whisper.

"Wouldn't you like to know," Ava taunted.

"What did he say?" I shouted, stepping forward, hands poised to grab her by the shoulders and shake the information out of her. Or maybe my hands were fixed in a position that would allow me to strangle the life out of her. The only thing I was certain of was the rage that consumed me.

I saw fear flash in her eyes, and like a predator, I advanced toward her menacingly. I had no idea what my intentions were, but I sensed weakness and moved swiftly in her direction—like an animal going after wounded prey.

"Don't touch me!" Ava shouted. She whirled around and tried to race to the elevator, but pregnancy slowed her down. I hastily pursued her, having no idea what I was going to do when I caught up with her.

"Get away from me, you crazy bitch," she shouted, looking over her shoulder as she jabbed the elevator button. The elevator doors opened slow and haltingly, giving me an opportunity to grab her by the back of the collar and yank her backward. But she jerked out of my grasp with such force she stumbled into the elevator and ran head-first into a wall.

She let out a yelp and her hands went up to her face. The bags from Starbucks crashed to the ground and the murky liquid of the Chai Latte spread across the elevator floor.

I ran in behind her and instantly turned up my nose. The rancid odor inside the elevator was overwhelming. It smelled like a public urinal. There was graffiti on the walls and cigarette butts littered the floor. My lips were scrunched together and my nose was turned up in disgust. As I tried to acclimate myself to the disgusting environment and foul odor, there was suddenly the sound of another enormous splash.

"Oh, shit! My water broke," Ava cried out. Bent over, she winced in pain as she cradled her bulging stomach.

Chapter 19

I gawked at the wet circle that stained her crotch, and then my gaze traveled down to the splatter of fluid that had intermingled with the hot beverage.

"What are you staring at? Call an ambulance!" Ava said bitterly.

I snapped out of my trancelike state and instinctually went into action. I darted over to her and began rubbing her back. "Don't worry; you're going to be all right," I said soothingly. "Listen, we shouldn't wait for an ambulance. We can get to the hospital quicker if I drive you."

"Okay," she whimpered.

"But...we need to get your coat and your phone from your apartment before we leave."

"That's true, I need my phone," she agreed, nodding briskly.

My mind was racing as I tried to come up with a plan. One thing I was certain of: I couldn't let Ava's phone get into the wrong hands. Not with multiple text messages connecting her to me.

"Your apartment is on the second floor, right?"

"Uh-huh." Ava's voice came out shaky and terrified.

Not wanting to touch the filthy elevator button with the pad of my finger, I poked it with my knuckle.

Ava flinched and cried out. "We need to hurry, Claire. This pain is starting to get to me."

"It's gonna be all right," I crooned, giving her a hug and stroking her horrendous green hair.

She moaned louder as the worn-down elevator jerkily ascended.

"Shh. Shh. Try to stay calm and try not to worry."

"Try not to worry? Oh really?" Her sarcasm was palpable.

"Stress isn't good for you or the baby," I said reasonably.

"My water broke and I'm holed up in the friggin' elevator with your crazy ass," she shouted in a high-pitched voice. She gasped suddenly, emitting a long croaking sound.

"Oh, God! It's too early for labor pains. Damn, I need my phone," she blurted angrily. "I have to call my friend, Walter and tell him to meet us at the hospital."

"Is Walter the older gentleman you were telling me about?" I asked, pretending not to know who she was referring to.

"Yeah."

"Why do you need him to meet you at the hospital?"

"That's none of your business," she said sharply as the elevator stopped on the second floor with a loud thud.

I linked my arm in hers and gently tried to guide her toward the door, but she backed into the corner of the elevator, refusing to budge.

"I can't walk; my stomach's cramping. Let me go," she said with insistence. Grimacing, she unlinked her arm from mine. She hunched over, her face contorted as she stuck a hand inside the pocket of her soggy sweat pants and pulled out a keyring. She handed it to me.

"Apartment two-fifteen?"

She nodded. "My phone is on the coffee table, and my coat—the one you bought me with the fur hood—is on a hook in the hall closet."

Before exiting the elevator, I hit the STOP button to prevent it from moving. I looked over my shoulder and saw Ava carefully lowering herself down to the squalid floor. Wincing and groaning, she took a seat amid the spilled food, murky water, and cigarette butts.

In pain or not, I would have forced myself to remain standing. No one could have paid me to sit in such filth and grime.

Searching for Ava's apartment, I headed down a hallway with lighting that flickered off and on. Surprisingly, two-fifteen had a welcome mat in front of the door and an attractive wreath hung above the apartment numbers.

Ava's apartment was small and sparsely furnished but neat as a pin. I spotted her phone on the coffee table, picked it up, and stuck it in my purse. Moving swiftly, I dashed to the hall closet and grabbed her coat.

Instead of rushing back to the elevator, I sat on the small couch that looked like it came from Ikea. My hands were shaking and I needed a moment to gather myself and think. It was paramount that I stop flying by the seat of my pants and come up with a definitive plan. Slumped over, I held my head in my trembling hands.

I wasn't sure if Ava was actually in labor or simply experiencing false contractions. From what I knew, premature rupture of the membranes didn't necessarily mean that contractions would follow. In some cases, women had their water break before their bodies were ready to start the labor process.

But how long did I have before Ava went into labor, if she hadn't already started?

She needed to get checked out by a doctor, for sure. But I couldn't take her to the hospital. If Walter was part of a clandestine organization, I couldn't let him get anywhere near Ava and the precious child she carried inside her womb.

Jesus, I was really losing it. My imagination was out of control. Walter was in his sixties. A retired senior citizen who enjoyed donating his time to worthy causes. Besides, he was too kind and giving to participate in a black market baby ring. Only the most vile and corrupt people were in the business of selling children.

Still, it would be foolish to underestimate him. If it turned out that he was actually involved in something sinister, I'd never forgive myself for being so naïve. I thought about the warning bells that went off in my head on the day I met him. I sensed that something wasn't right with him, but I couldn't pinpoint it. And I still couldn't.

Just in case my suspicions were true, it was imperative that I stay two steps ahead of him.

But how?

Suddenly aware that Ava might find the strength to flee the elevator, I jumped to my feet and raced out of the apartment.

Panting, I rushed inside the elevator and luckily, she was exactly where I'd left her—a heap in the corner, on the floor.

"I'm back," I said breathlessly. "Are you feeling any better?"

"Not really. The cramping stopped, but now my back is killing me."

"Don't worry, I can get you to the hospital in ten minutes." I helped her to her feet and draped her coat over her shoulders. I restarted the elevator and placed my arm around her in a way that appeared protective, but I was actually keeping her close to me—just in case she became suspicious of my intentions and tried to break away.

In the parking lot, I looked around to see if there were any cameras. I didn't see any and doubted if such a rundown place had any cameras that operated properly. Carefully escorting Ava to the car, I hit the keypad, unlocking the doors. I helped her into the backseat and urged her to lie down.

"It's so cold," she muttered as she tried to curl up.

"Oh, what was I thinking? I should have picked up a dry pair of pants for you when I was in your apartment. If you'd like, I can go back up."

"No, that's okay. Just get me to the hospital." Using her coat as a makeshift blanket, she covered her torso area.

Remembering that I had something that would cover Ava's whole body, I popped open the trunk and retrieved the blanket that Jeff and I had used when we went on a picnic in the park last summer.

Oh, Jeff! I had so many sweet memories of him. He'd given me so much joy. How could my life have gone from such blissful rapture to a complete, living Hell? It suddenly hit me, how much I missed him. How much I yearned for the feeling of his strong arm enfolding me.

"Hurry up, let's go," Ava called from the car. I pushed thoughts of Jeff out of my mind. There was no time for sweet reminiscing when I had to deal with the wretchedness of my current reality.

I gingerly placed the chilled blanket over Ava's waist, covering up the wetness that soaked her tights.

"This blanket is freezing," she complained.

"I know. I'm sorry. It'll warm up soon." I closed the back door of the car and hurriedly got behind the wheel. I started the engine and turned the heat on full blast.

"Oh, the heat feels good," Ava said with a contented moan. It was the first agreeable comment I'd ever heard her speak.

I pulled out of the lot and began driving in the opposite direction of the hospital, hoping Ava wouldn't notice. She didn't utter a word of complaint, and after a few minutes of uncharacteristic silence, I peeked in the rearview mirror to check on her. To my surprise, she was huddled in a ball, fast asleep.

I let out a long breath of relief.

Trying to figure out what to do with her, I drove aimlessly for a few miles. Basically, I was kidnapping Ava, and it was the craziest thing I'd ever done. So crazy, it felt surreal. I kept checking the rearview mirror to make sure she was still asleep. I had no idea how I would respond if she woke up and became confrontational.

I was panicked by the idea that if I got caught, I could do hard time in prison. The very thought of being behind bars sent a chill up my spine.

As I drove in circles, I got an idea. I could take Ava to my cabin in the mountains. I hadn't visited the cabin in over a year, and for all I knew, the place could be overrun with squirrels, raccoons, and other forest creatures. But I didn't have a choice. The cabin was in a remote area. Secluded. The perfect place to hide out.

It was a two-hour trip and with only a quarter tank of gas, I had to pull into the first service station I saw. While filling the tank, I peered through the window, keeping a watchful eye on Ava.

Back in the car, I feared the sound of the engine turning would awaken her, but she didn't budge from her curled position. I would have loved to listen to the radio during the long drive, but I feared the sound might disturb her.

With only the hum of the engine keeping me company, I headed for the highway.

As I sped along the open road of the highway, my anxiety began to ease up. I was no longer concerned about Ava waking up. What could she do at this point—scream, cry, curse at me? She was officially my captive. Once we arrived in the mountains, I'd probably have to drag her kicking and screaming into the cabin.

Then a sudden, farfetched idea occurred to me. I could force her into the cabin at gunpoint. The police had returned Brandon's murder weapon to Howard, the rightful owner, so I didn't actually have access to a gun. But I was sure I could trick her into believing that the stun gun inside the console was a real one.

I was going to get her in that cabin by any means necessary. Even if my suspicions were wrong and she didn't plan on selling the baby... even if she had the good intention of raising it herself, I still refused to allow a sociopath like Ava the opportunity to ruin an innocent life.

It concerned me that her water had broken. She'd probably go into labor within the next forty-eight hours. I was grateful that the baby wouldn't need to be placed in an incubator since it was determined at the last ultrasound that he already weighed four pounds.

I'd done a lot of research on childbirth when I was carrying Brandon and I'd learned that a preterm, low-birthweight infant required an incubator until it was able to maintain a stable body temperature, typically at three pounds. My grandson was out of the woods in that regard.

Although I wasn't qualified to deliver a baby, desperate times called for desperate measures. You could find anything on the Internet, and there was no doubt in my mind that someone had posted childbirth instructions online. Unfortunately, I'd shut off the cable and Wi-Fi at the cabin. Instead of using my laptop to go online, I'd have to rely on the smaller cell phone screen.

Hopefully, I'd be able to get a signal on my phone.

Trying not to focus on the sheer lunacy of my plan, I directed my attention to the road ahead.

"Where're we going?" Ava's voice, scratchy from sleep, cut into the quiet.

"We're on our way to the hospital," I said, injecting warmth into my tone.

"Why're we on the turnpike?" she asked, propping herself up and looking out the window.

"Uh..." My mind raced, searching for a plausible answer. Unable to come up with anything, I accelerated.

Ava leaned forward, squeezing between the two front seats as she stared warily through the windshield. "What's going on, Claire? Where're you taking me?"

"I'm taking you to the hospital." I'd tried to sound as sincere as possible, but my tone rang false.

"Where's my phone?" she demanded, patting her pockets.

"It's in your coat pocket."

She scooted back and rifled through the pockets of her coat. "I can't find it." Her voice was shrill with panic. "I don't know what kind of game you're playing, but I want to get out of this car. I'm not kidding," she shouted.

"You're getting yourself worked up over nothing; now relax, hon," I said soothingly.

"Listen, you crazy bitch, get off at the next exit and take me home! Or call nine-one-one and let an ambulance take me to a hospital. I should have known better than to get in this car with you."

As Ava ranted and raved, my eyes darted back and forth from the highway to the rearview mirror, monitoring her and bracing myself for any sudden moves on her part. I was prepared to elbow her, hard, if she tried anything crazy.

She jiggled the door handle. "Fuck!" She cursed bitterly when she realized the child lock was engaged. She didn't strike me as someone with a death wish, but in case I was wrong, I picked up speed in an attempt to deter her from reaching for the steering wheel and deliberately trying to cause us to crash.

She went into an angry rage and began screaming and accusing me of confiscating her phone. When I ignored her, she became frustrated and began punching the back of the empty passenger's seat.

"Ava, I'm asking you nicely to stop acting like a child. Please stop yelling in my ear; sit back, and relax."

"How do you expect me to relax when you've got me in the middle of nowhere? Do you think I want to have this baby in the backseat of your freakin' car?" she hollered, her voice bordering on hysterical.

"You're not going to have the baby in the car. You're not even in labor," I said reasonably. And although I was an emotional wreck, too, I managed to keep my voice steady and calm.

"You're a nutcase, lady. You're fucking crazy—just like your son!"

Suddenly, I flipped open the center console and retrieved the stun gun. Ava gasped and recoiled.

"I'll show you crazy. If you dare to open your mouth and speak disparagingly of my son, again, I will put a twenty-two in your thigh. It won't kill you, but it'll hurt like hell. Cutting it out of your flesh will hurt even worse. So, if I were you, I'd keep my mouth shut for the rest of the trip."

For a moment, she looked as if she might say something else, but then thought better of it and sank back in her seat. Watching her in the rearview mirror, I could see her eyes glistening with tears.

I was in control now, and the feeling of power was exhilarating.

Chapter 20

Ava alternately stared through the side window for a while, and then would switch her gaze to the rear window, looking longingly at the highway signs that we passed in a flash. We'd been riding in silence for about forty minutes when it dawned on me that I could turn on the radio now that she was fully awake.

Music had always been a comfort to me and I found a station playing a tribute to Prince. I hummed along to "Little Red Corvette" as I sped down the highway.

"I have to go to the bathroom." Ava's voice was meek and quiet.

"You'll have to hold it until we get there."

"Get where?"

"That's none of your business!"

"I have a right to know where you're taking me," she said sharply. Her ability to be quiet and humble had been short-lived and she was back to being mean and feisty.

"Why are you doing this? What do you want from me?" She went quiet briefly and then her eyes widened with incredulity. "Oh, my God...you want my baby?"

"Someone has to raise him right. And that someone is not you,

Ava. You're not fit to be a mother, and we both are keenly aware of that fact."

"I'm not trying to be a mother. He's already set to go to a good home. I met the parents and they seem like really nice people."

"Ah! Now the truth comes out," I said, shaking my head. "What's in it for you, Ava? How much are you getting paid?"

"Nothing," she said indignantly. "The agency only pays my expenses—they don't give me anything extra."

"Do you really expect me to believe that you deliberately got pregnant so you could help a childless couple?" I asked, my voice warbled and high. "Give me a break," I spat. "I should have known when Brandon told me about your sudden desire to have a child, that it was nothing more than a money scheme." I grunted in disgust. "You are the most despicable human being I've ever known."

"Whatever. But I still have to pee," she said defiantly. "And I need to get out these wet pants before I get sick."

For a brief moment, I felt compelled to find her a dry pair of pants. I checked the time, and although it was getting late, stores like Walmart or Target were likely to be open until around ten. I dug my phone out of my bag to search for the location of the nearest Walmart, but changed my mind. Ava didn't deserve any kindness from me. Not after the way she'd mistreated Brandon and used him for stud service. He'd been nothing more than a sperm donor and a source of income for her. She'd coldheartedly driven a deeply troubled young man over the edge, yet she expected me to turn the other cheek and be compassionate.

"You don't get it, Ava," I said with steel in my voice.

"I don't get what?" she asked irritably.

"You want me to care about your wet pants and your health, but what you need to understand is that your comfort and well-being don't concern me."

The weeks that I'd had to pretend to like Ava had taken a toll on my psyche. Being able to finally speak my truth was liberating.

"Are you saying you don't care if I piss all over this nice leather seat back here?" she inquired, smirking as she ran a hand over the seat.

She had me. I cared about my car seat being soaked with urine and having to inhale the stench for the duration of the drive. I slowed down, then pulled over to the shoulder that ran along the side of dense woods. "Get out."

Ava looked around warily at the pitch-blackness. "This isn't a rest stop. I'm not peeing out there in the dark, freezing cold."

I unlocked the doors and got out of the car. I yanked open the rear door. "Get out," I repeated through clenched teeth, pointing the stun gun at her.

"Crazy, fucking bitch," she muttered scornfully as she put her coat on and reluctantly climbed out.

I stood guard as she tussled with her coat and wet pants, cursing as she tried to pull the pants down while holding the coat up around her waist. After struggling to position herself in a wide-leg squat, she urinated for what seemed like a full ten minutes.

"I need tissue paper," she said crossly.

"Our ancestors used leaves," I informed her with a snide smile.

"This is so fucked up. It's so fucking fucked up!"

"And how do you suppose Brandon felt?" I asked in a monotone. "You can't begin to imagine how hopeless he must have felt when he put that gun to his head."

"I didn't have anything to do with what he did. He was a messed-up person."

I shot her a look.

"I'm sorry that I can't speak of your son in glowing terms, but the way he offed himself—over an argument—was stupid."

I looked at her contemptuously.

She shrugged. "All I'm saying is what he did to himself is proof that he was a head case," she said, her vicious words emerging without emotion.

Clearly, Ava had no empathy for others and took no responsibility for Brandon's tragic death. She preyed on weakness and that was all the more reason to get a helpless baby away from her.

"Sounds to me like you handpicked Brandon for your scheme. You carefully chose someone with self-esteem issues to father your child—a fragile soul that could be easily manipulated. Sure, Brandon had his faults, but he was innocent. No match for a conniving street-smart girl like you. No doubt, he was devastated to learn that you'd only kept him around until you got a positive pregnancy test. Am I right?"

She didn't respond. Instead she stepped out of her slippers. She gasped when her bare feet touched the frosted ground.

I rolled my eyes in annoyance. "What are you doing?"

"I have to get out of these wet pants. I'm not catching pneumonia for you or anyone else."

"Wet clothes don't cause pneumonia, you moron!"

"What are you, a doctor or something?"

She had a lot of balls to keep getting sarcastic with me while I was holding what she believed to be a gun. "I'm not going to tell you again... get back in the car."

Defiant, she flung the sweat pants into the snow-covered bushes.

"Pick them up," I said with authority. "You can't go out in public without any pants on."

"Are we going to a public place?" She sounded hopeful.

I ignored the question. "Just get the damn pants."

Sulking like an ornery preschooler, Ava stomped over to the bushes and retrieved the sweats. I tossed them in the trunk, figuring I'd wash and dry them when we arrived at the cabin. There were old clothes of mine and Brandon's there, but nothing that would fit a pregnant person.

We got back in the car and Ava wrapped herself up in the blanket and lay down. I hoped she'd fall asleep again, but no such luck. Five minutes later, she popped upright. "I'm freezing. Can you turn up the heat?"

Accommodating her, I cranked the heat up as high as it would go. The temperature in the car became uncomfortably warm, but I endured the discomfort because I was tired of hearing her complaints.

I'd always done my best thinking while driving, and I had to figure out a way to keep Ava confined once we reached the cabin. I didn't have any handcuffs or a chain to lock her down, but I thought there might be some rope somewhere in the cabin. But what good would it do when I had no idea how to tie a secure knot?

I could lock her in the main bathroom, I supposed. Yes, that was a great idea. It would be as if she were in solitary confinement, where she deserved to be.

It took a really evil and heartless person to deliberately bring a child into the world for the sole purpose of selling it. It nauseated me to think of what could have happened to my grandchild had I not intervened.

We had another hour to go, and I felt much better now that I had a concrete plan. Ava would give birth in the bathtub or on the floor if she preferred. Hopefully, the baby wouldn't need medical attention. If he seemed to be okay after he was born, I'd drop Ava off in the woods and let her fend for herself and then immediately charter a flight out of the country.

There was something incredibly peaceful about driving on a highway at night. Ava was finally quiet in the backseat, which was a nice change. Slow jams from the '90s played on the radio, reminding me of my teen years. Instead of feeling nostalgically regretful as I normally did whenever I heard music from my youth, I felt serene and hopeful about the future.

"Ohhh," Ava suddenly moaned from the backseat.

"What's wrong?"

"I just got a bad pain. A really bad one. I think I'm in labor."

"Are you sure?"

"I don't know. I think so."

"Okay, let's time the contractions." I was surprised by my own calmness, but I realized it wouldn't be helpful if Ava and I both became hysterical.

I'd hoped she wouldn't go into labor for a few days, giving me time to get the cabin in order and to pick up a cradle and other items for the baby. But babies come when they're ready, not when it's convenient.

"Oh, my God, here comes another one." Ava reared back and yelled at the top of her lungs.

"The closest hospital is about fifty miles from here. I need you to try to be calm until we get there."

"Don't tell me to calm down," she shouted and then took her frustration out on the passenger's seat, slapping the headrest and kicking the back of the seat.

"The way you're acting, I can't tell if you're throwing a tantrum or if you're experiencing an authentic contraction," I said in an even tone of voice.

"Ooooo. Ahh! This fucking hurts so baaad! You gotta take me to the hospital. I'm not kidding. Get off the goddamn highway, right now! I need medical attention, you bitch!"

Although Ava was freaking out, and the loud shrieking was driving me batty, I managed to remain calm. I had to. I couldn't take her to a hospital and risk her contacting the people from the agency, and so I continued driving at a moderate speed, looking straight ahead with my eyes on the road.

Childbearing was a normal part of life, I reminded myself. Women had been delivering children without any help since the beginning of time.

"Please, Claire. Help me." Trying to cope with being in active labor, Ava began blowing out short bursts of air through her mouth, using the Lamaze breathing technique. I was sure Ava was only mimicking what she'd seen pregnant women do on TV and in the movies. I found it hard to believe that she'd ever bothered to take a Lamaze class. In fact, I found it highly unlikely that she'd ever heard of Lamaze.

Yanking on the overhead hand grip, she howled in pain for an extended period and then whimpered pitifully as the contraction subsided.

"Why are you doing this to me?" Her voice was shrill. "I don't want to have a baby in a goddamned car. Look, I won't tell anyone that you kidnapped me. I swear, I won't. And I'll give you the baby as soon as we're released from the hospital. My word is my bond. You can trust me, Claire."

I could trust *her*? That was a laugh. She'd say anything while she was in agony. She'd plead, bargain, and make all sorts of promises that she didn't intend to keep. The only way Ava would willingly hand her infant over to me was if I offered to pay her more money than the agency had. She was flat-out lying when she'd said that they were only paying her expenses. It wasn't logical that a greedy, lazy, and morally corrupt individual like Ava would endure a pregnancy merely for living expenses.

One way or another, I'd get the truth out of her. Agonizing pain motivated people to tell the truth.

"Oh, no! It's happening again!" Ava exclaimed with her face contorted. This time she yanked on the hand grip in sync with the Lamaze breathing, interspersed with piteous moans.

Whatever works for you, Ava, I thought sardonically.

Her contractions were close. From my estimation, they seemed to be coming every three to five minutes. From personal experience, I knew the contractions could continue at the current pace and intensity for another few hours.

We had another forty minutes or so until we reached the cabin, and in the meantime, there was nothing I could do for her except concentrate on driving and not allow her screams to cause me to run off the road.

Experiencing a short break from the pain, Ava wedged herself between the two front seats, in an attempt to reason with me. "Think about your grandson, Claire. This isn't healthy for him. And it's not fair to *me!* It wasn't supposed to go down like this. I was promised a pain-free childbirth experience. At this moment I should be chilling in the hospital with good drugs and nice nurses taking care of me."

"I understand...it's all about you," I said sarcastically.

"That's not true; I'm also thinking about my son. He deserves better than this. He's going to be a preemie and tiny babies need incubators and should be under a doctor's care."

It wasn't as if she really gave a damn about her child, so I didn't bother to explain that the baby already had sufficient weight to be placed in an open crib. "The baby will be fine," I said, leaving it at that.

"How do you know he'll be fine? You're not a doctor." She sighed in exasperation and dropped her head in her hands. When she lifted it, I noticed the muscles in her face beginning to twitch.

"Uh-oh, you better grab that hand grip, again," I said tauntingly, giving her a taste of how it felt to be ridiculed when you were in dire pain. Like Brandon had been when she'd taunted him in those text messages. I didn't have an ounce of sympathy for what Ava was going through. In fact, I was enjoying it.

Chapter 21

"Aaaaaah," Ava wailed. "Something's happening. Stop the car! This fucking baby is trying to come out of me. I'm serious. His head! It's like...right there. Trying to come out!"

"It's good to know he's in the right position," I said calmly. "Now, lie down. You don't want the baby's head to hit the floor when you push him out."

She wiggled onto her back, but kept thrashing. "Claire, you have to pull over and call a damn ambulance!"

Traffic had thinned out and there were hardly any cars on the highway. I didn't want to pull over and draw attention to us. All I wanted was to get to the cabin as quickly as possible, and so I kept driving.

"Why won't you help me?" Ava hissed.

"I have to get us where we're going. Pulling over won't stop the baby from coming. Furthermore, women don't actually need assistance during childbirth. Hospital births are merely another way for the medical profession to make money."

"Fuck you, bitch!" she exploded, giving me the finger. "I bet you had your baby in a goddamn hospital," she raged.

"Lie back and push, Ava."

"Hell, no," she screamed. "I'm not pushing; I don't want to have my baby like this. Oh, my God, this is horrible. Oh, oh, oh. Aaaaah. Argghh. Ah, ah, ah."

As pain consumed her again, she moved from one end of the back-seat to the other. Some of the sounds that emerged from Ava barely sounded human. In between the pains, she cursed at me passionately, but I kept my cool and continued driving within the speed limit. The last thing I wanted to do was alert the state police by speeding or driving erratically.

"I'm scared," she whimpered in a child's voice and for a moment, my heart went out to her. But remembering her intention to sell the baby like he was a commodity hardened my heart. Needing to know all the facts and the full truth, I decided to manipulate her.

"Ava, there's a hospital coming up in three miles."

"Really?" The relief in her voice was palpable.

"Yes, but I need you to give me your word that you'll let me have my grandson."

"You can have him. I swear...I promise."

"I don't believe you."

"I'm telling the truth."

"I don't think you'll give him to me without money. So tell me how much the agency promised to pay you and I'll top it."

"Well, you know, it's not really an agency. It's just these three guys. I only deal with one of them. The older man I told you about...Walter."

My heart pounded in my chest. Veronica had no idea the kind of man she was dealing with.

"They're going to give me twenty-thousand dollars once I deliver a healthy baby." She paused and winced. "Oh, God. Please drive faster."

"You don't want us to get pulled over, do you?"

"Do you think I fucking care?" she bellowed.

"Okay, calm down. Don't get upset. Listen, I'll give you thirty thousand. Will you accept it?"

"Sure." She smiled despite the pain and her eyes twinkled with greed.

Another contraction took the smile off Ava's face and sent her into another whirlwind of anguish. When she caught her breath, I continued questioning her.

"Were these men actually going to allow you to give birth in a reputable hospital?" I asked doubtfully.

"Not exactly. Walter was going to take me to a birthing center with a doula. But the center offered good drugs and good nursing care just like a hospital."

"I see," I said as I zipped past an exit.

Mouth agape, Ava gawked out the window. "Hey, why'd you drive past the exit?"

"Oh, I'm sorry. I was so caught up in hearing about this baby-selling ring, I missed the exit. No worries, I'll take the next one."

"Are you fucking kidding me? How long is that gonna be?"

"Only a few more minutes."

"A few minutes is too long. Christ! You have to help me! His head is coming out. I can feel it. Oh, shit. This baby is coming out. Oh, my God. I can't do this. I can't do this, I can't do this," she repeated like a mantra.

"You can do it, Ava. Try to relax. Okay? Just relax," I coaxed.

"I can't relax," she roared. "You have to get me out this car! Oh, God, please, please. I need a doctor to help me."

Ava started yelling without cessation and it was hard to maintain my composure. Checking on her through the mirror, I wasn't comfortable with what I was seeing. She was sitting on the edge of the seat, screaming like a banshee. From my vantage point, it appeared that she was going to let the baby plop out and fall head-first onto the floor. Not trusting that her motherly instincts would kick in and prompt her to catch him, I pulled over on the shoulder of the road and screeched to a stop.

"It's coming. It's coming out right now," Ava yelled as I jumped in the backseat. I prayed that a well-meaning trooper wouldn't stop to provide assistance. She was freaking out, but I managed to get her to lie down so I could help deliver the baby. I expected to see the head crowning and was utterly surprised to find that the baby's entire head was already out. Moments later, the shoulders emerged and the rest of the baby literally plopped out—into my hands. I quickly wrapped him in the blanket that Ava had been using, and I wiped his little face and head with another portion of the blanket.

His cry was music to my ears, relieving me of having to worry about suctioning him.

As Ava lay on her back panting, I placed him on her chest, covered with the blanket. "You have to hold him. When we get there, I'll cut the cord."

All the fight was out of Ava. She didn't protest or argue with me. She didn't curse or scream. She simply placed an arm over the baby and sobbed as I drove to the cabin.

Naked from the waist down beneath her three-quarter-length coat, Ava carried the newborn. Before getting out of the car, I'd made sure he was bundled snugly inside the large blanket.

With her legs gapped from the placenta that had yet to expel, Ava took cautious steps, the rubber soles of her slippers crunching on the hardened snow. It wasn't likely that she'd run off into the cold night, but in case she had any clever ideas, I kept a strong grip on her arm.

Using the flashlight on my phone to illuminate the way, I slowly and carefully guided her along the icy pebbled path that led to the cabin. "Hold the baby tight and watch your step," I warned.

The isolated cabin was off the main road and the closest neighbor was about three miles away. Shrouded by large trees, the cabin was a glorious sight in the sunlight, but in the dark of night, it had a foreboding appearance and the trees cast ominous shadows.

"Where are we?" Oddly, Ava didn't sound afraid. She sounded sedate. Defeated and weary.

"We're home," I said brusquely. All the anger I'd felt toward Ava had dissipated now that the baby had arrived, but I had to keep up my tough-guy act to ensure her cooperation.

I opened the door and groped for the light switch when the automated voice of the alarm system sounded. The light flickered on and I smiled as I punched in the code and disarmed the system. Thankfully I'd kept up the utilities payments at the cabin, but I could only hope that the water pipes weren't frozen.

Ava looked around. I could tell by her expression that she was relieved that there was electricity and modern furnishings.

She lingered near the front door as if contemplating making a run for it.

I pointed to the couch. "Sit."

She obeyed, hobbling over to the couch, but her eyes kept darting to the door.

I armed the alarm and locked the door from the inside. Satisfied that Ava wasn't going anywhere, I walked over to the couch and hovered over her and the baby. I lifted the blanket from his face and smiled down at him.

"It's freezing in here," she said in a trembling voice. She glanced at the fireplace with trepidation. "Do you have, like, wood or logs or whatever for that thing?"

I ignored her question and walked briskly to the thermostat in the hall and turned on the heat. The rumbling of the heating unit coming to life was a welcomed sound.

Realizing that it could take up to an hour for the cabin to heat up,

I grabbed some folded blankets from the master bedroom closet and then went to the laundry room that was off from the kitchen, and tossed them in the dryer. Heated blankets would help with the baby's body temperature.

I returned to the living room at the very moment that the placenta expelled from Ava's body. She let out a yelp when it plopped to the floor.

"Ew! What is that?" She kicked the bloodied mass of tissue, grimacing as if an alien had popped out of her body. She tried to scoot away from it, and cowered in the corner of the couch. She looked confused when she found herself pulling it along with her.

Judging by the limp way Ava held the baby as she scowled at the placenta, it was obvious that childbirth hadn't instilled an ounce of motherly instinct in her.

"Didn't you read anything about childbirth during your pregnancy?" I asked with disgust.

"What for? That's what doctors and doulas go to school for."

I rolled my eyes heavenward. "That thing on the floor is called the placenta. It's how the fetus is fed during pregnancy, and it'll stay attached to the baby until the cord is cut."

"Well, what are you waiting for? Cut it already!"

"Sit still," I said and rushed to the kitchen and retrieved a plastic trash liner from a pack in a drawer. In the main room, while Ava kept her head turned in the opposite direction of the placenta, I lifted it and placed it inside the trash liner.

Making a face, she stole a glance at me. "Why're you doing that? Do you plan on keeping that nasty thing?"

"For a while."

"Why?" Ava shrank back, looking horrified.

"When the cord is left attached to the baby until it falls off by itself—usually in about four to ten days—the baby can absorb all the nutrients the placenta has to give. And this little fellow needs all the additional nutrients he can get."

"What he needs is a hospital instead of your voodoo methods of taking care of him," Ava said sassily.

"Don't pretend to care about that baby," I admonished. "I don't need to explain anything to a heartless tramp, willing to sell the precious human life that she brought into the world, but I'll educate you anyway."

I had hoped to wound her with my words, but if I thought calling Ava a heartless tramp would get a reaction out of her, I was wrong. She looked at me stone-faced and didn't as much as flinch.

Feeling a bit let down, I went on with the explanation. "More and more, women are returning to home births, and they're respecting that nature's perfection is better than man's technology. The holistic way to give birth is to simply let it happen."

"That's a crock of shit and easy for you to say. I bet you didn't respect nature's perfection and allow yourself to put up with the hellish pain you let me go through. A prissy chick like you would have demanded a shitload of drugs the moment you felt that first pain."

"That's partly true, but if I had it to do over again—"

"Yeah, yeah, yeah. Whatever." Cutting me off, Ava stood up, causing the plastic-covered placenta to drag a little. She looked down at it sneeringly. "Is it okay if I, like, go to the bathroom?"

"Sure, it's at the end of the hall." I took the baby from her arms. Free of the baby and the placenta, visible relief washed over Ava.

Bare-legged and clutching her coat around her, Ava walked stiffly in the direction of the hallway. I noticed her footsteps falter when she eyed a landline phone on an end table near the hallway.

"Don't even think about it," I warned. "Anyway, it's disconnected."

"How long are you gonna keep me here?" she asked, sounding forlorn.

"As long as necessary."

"What does that mean? I don't understand why you're still holding me hostage. I said you could have the baby; what more do you want?" Her voice cracked and her bottom lip quivered, and she looked on the verge of begging me for her freedom.

But I needed her here...for the baby. And since I didn't owe her an explanation, I simply pointed to the hallway.

Ava stood there for another second, looking at me with pleading eyes.

I could barely look at her, she looked so terrible. Her face was streaked with dried tears, and her awful green hair had become a medusa-like mass of tangles.

When she finally gave up on begging me with her eyes, she turned and shuffled out of the living room, and that's when I noticed that blood and other gook had dried on the insides of her legs.

"There're washcloths and towels in the bathroom cabinet," I called after her.

She turned around. "What about sanitary napkins; do you have any?"

I shook my head. "But there's plenty of toilet tissue."

She sighed. "What about a pair of sweats or jeans. Can I at least cover up? Can I have some dignity?"

"I'll look around and see what's here when you finish in the bathroom. Oh, the water's probably still cold. It'll be a while before it heats up."

Ava muttered something under her breath and ambled away.

Carrying the baby, I went to the laundry room and took a warm blanket out and held it up to my face, making sure it wasn't too warm. I wrapped it around the blanket the baby was already enfolded inside and then sat on the couch.

He wriggled inside the snug blanket as I rocked my little bundle of joy, calming him. "Are you warm, sweetie? I bet my little man is nice and toasty, now," I cooed.

Alone with the baby, I pulled back the cover and took another look at his face. I marveled at how much he looked like Brandon did as a newborn. Even with his little face encrusted with remnants of afterbirth, and with his eyes closed, the resemblance to Brandon was startling.

I was awestruck by the immense love that I felt for the child. Though not a religious person, I couldn't help from perceiving him as a blessing and a gift from God.

"Hello, Brandon," I whispered and held him close to my heart. "Oh, I can't wait to get you cleaned up and dressed in a cute outfit and on a plane out of here." I rocked him lovingly. "Can you open those pretty eyes for me, Bran?" I cooed.

He responded by squirming in my arms and squeezing his eyes closed even tighter.

I laughed but inwardly hoped he didn't turn out as temperamental as his father. And God forbid if he took after his mean-spirited mother.

Chapter 22

When Ava returned to the main room, I handed her the baby. "Feed him while I look for something for you to put on."

"What am I supposed to feed him? Do you have formula or bottles around here?"

"Are you deliberately being an idiot, Ava?" I asked impatiently. "Pull up your top and try to get him to latch onto your nipple. It's not rocket science."

"I'm not breastfeeding this baby. I didn't sign up for that."

"Shut up and sit down."

She flopped down on the couch.

"Be careful with him," I said sharply.

"I'm not breastfeeding the kid. I don't want my boobs to hang down to my tummy."

"Surgery will fix you up. You're looking forward to going under the knife, aren't you?"

Ava laughed mirthlessly. "I can't believe I went through all of this for nothing. And all I have to show for it is a messed-up body. It's not fair."

"I'd love to be entertained by your little pity party, but the baby needs colostrum."

"He needs what?"

"Your milk hasn't come in yet. That'll take a few days, but in the meantime, there's a small amount of a sticky yellow fluid building in your breasts."

A look of distaste crossed Ava's face. "Ew," she uttered, frowning down at her chest.

"That fluid is filled with important antibodies, and the baby needs the extra protection from those antibodies."

She stood up, like she'd heard enough and intended to leave. "Sorry, I didn't sign up for all this. I'm not comfortable with the idea of being sucked on like a cow. All the kid needs is some formula. That's what normal babies drink."

The kid. It was the second time she'd used that impersonal expression, reminding me of the insulting way Howard had referred to Brandon his entire life. Suddenly filled with a fiery rage, I stepped toward Ava with my palm raised. "If you ever call this baby, 'the kid,' again, I'll slap the hell out of you and then shoot you in the leg *and* the ankle."

Ava looked at me as if I'd lost my mind. "Jesus, you're bugging out over nothing. It's not that serious."

"It's serious to me. His name is Brandon. Bran for short. Do not refer to him as *the kid!*"

"Okay, whatever." Ava shrugged a shoulder.

Frankly, Ava baffled me. One moment she acted frightened and shaky, and the next, she was smug and arrogant. I was getting fed up with her attitude, and wished I really did have a real gun with bullets.

"I'm not going to ask you twice." I patted my handbag, reminding her of the alleged gun I was carrying. "You have two choices: feel the discomfort of feeding Bran or the agony of having a bullet cut out of your leg. As far as your ankle..." I let my words trail off ominously. "The bullet would probably shatter the bone and cause you to walk with a limp." Mimicking her, I gave a nonchalant shrug.

Looking pissed off, she sat back down. I sat next to her, reached over and tugged at her top.

"I don't need any help. I got it," she said agitatedly, pushing my hand away. She held Bran in the crook of her left arm and awkwardly tried to pull up the stretchy fabric with her free hand.

"Let me help," I spoke more gently.

"I said, I got it," she insisted.

Babies picked up on negativity, and I didn't want there to be any unnecessary tension between Ava and me. For the sake of Bran's emotional well-being, I backed off.

She yanked her bra up. "Right or left boob?"

"It doesn't matter. Start with either one, and then switch him to the other."

She positioned the baby's mouth near her nipple and winced when he latched on and began suckling.

"Ugh! This is so disgusting. How long is he going to need this colostomy stuff?"

"Colostrum," I corrected. "He'll need to be fed by you for about four or five days."

"You can't expect me to stick around here—in the middle of nowhere—for that long."

"Your wants don't concern me, Ava," I said coldly.

"I can't believe you're making me feed him some yellow mess I never heard of, and you're saving that nasty-looking placenta like it's something sacred. This sucks...it's so, so, so fucked up."

"No, *you're* fucked up!" I didn't want to argue with her in front of Bran, but I couldn't hold back my feelings. I glared at her. "Do you have any idea what happens to babies that are sold on the black market?"

"They go to good homes with decent parents?"

"Sometimes...if they're lucky. But in many instances, the commissioning couple has a change of heart and doesn't show up when the baby's born. In such cases, the orphaned infant is available to be purchased by anyone who can afford the new, discounted price. Sickos, pornographers, and child molesters can get their hands on an innocent child and do whatever they want with it because of greedy, selfish people like you."

If I thought my spiel would strike a chord within Ava and appeal to her sense of human decency, I was wrong.

She stared at me blankly. "Are you gonna get me something to wear or what?"

"Switch him to the other breast," I said in exasperation.

She wasn't putting forth much effort in trying to get the baby to suck and I didn't care if she felt offended or not, I took it upon myself to assist in getting her other nipple into Bran's mouth.

I watched like a hawk and didn't leave the room in search of clothing for her until after Bran had stopped suckling and had fallen asleep.

As I passed Brandon's room, I averted my gaze. I didn't have the heart to look inside and see the things he'd left behind the last time he was here—which would have been when he was around fifteen or sixteen. I couldn't bear to see signs of Brandon back when he was a teenager and not quite as cynical and unhappy with life.

Back when I might have been able to help him if I hadn't listened to the so-called experts.

Hanging in my bedroom closet was a pair of powder-blue jeans with an elastic waist. The jeans weren't my style and I couldn't recall buying them, but there they were, nevertheless.

When I handed them to Ava, along with a pair of socks, and a loose-fitting white top, she turned up her nose.

"Mom jeans," she said disgustedly. "I guess I'm really an adult now."

I ignored the sarcasm. "Are you hungry, Ava?"

"Starving."

"There's nothing in the fridge, but I'll see what's in the cabinets."

"I was thinking more like, Chick-fil-A or maybe getting a fat, juicy Whopper and some fries from the drive-thru at Burger King."

"That's not happening," I said and strode to the kitchen.

In one of the cabinets, I found an unopened box of pancake mix that only required water. There was also a bag of rice, a container of vegetable oil, a bottle of syrup, random canned goods and other miscellaneous items that I could use to whip together a few meals.

Ava made a face when I presented her with a plate of pancakes and syrup with spinach and green beans on the side.

"Make sure you eat the veggies. For the baby," I added.

If I had my way, I would have put Ava on an organic diet, ensuring that Bran was nourished properly. Unfortunately, processed food with all kinds of nasty preservatives was all that was available for the time being.

The cabin was finally warm and cozy. Ava turned the TV on and was not pleased to discover the cable wasn't connected.

I offered her a stack of DVDs. Most of them had belonged to Brandon.

"Look at this shit. There's nothing worth watching," she complained as she shuffled through the selection, which consisted mostly of Japanese anime and sci-fi movies. She grudgingly settled on *Avatar*.

Although I was looking at the TV screen, I wasn't paying attention to what was going on. My mind raced in different directions, trying to decide if I should fly to Mexico before going to France. In Mexico I could get Bran a medical examination without having to answer a million questions. And for the right price, I could probably purchase a new identity.

As my mind wandered, I thought about my employer. What would they think when I didn't show up for work in the morning? Would it be presumed that I'd experienced another mental collapse? Maybe I should call and pretend I'd come down with a bad case of the flu. Better to give a flimsy explanation than allow my colleagues to draw their own salacious conclusions.

I glanced over at Bran and smiled. He was sleeping in a bureau drawer that I'd padded with a blanket. The plastic-wrapped placenta rested at the foot of the homemade crib.

He wore a diaper that I had fashioned from a T-shirt that boasted, *Always Better In the Poconos.* Although the sides were enclosed with safety pins, the diaper still fit so loosely, it threatened to slide right off of him.

With the huge amount of brand-new baby clothes that I'd purchased for Bran, it was ironic that he was dressed like a ragamuffin. Unfortunately, I couldn't risk going back to my house, and those adorable items, so carefully selected, would never be worn. But as soon as we were safely out of the area, I planned to buy him piles and piles of new clothing, and everything his heart could desire.

When Bran cried, Ava didn't budge or bat an eye. She sulked and cast a glance of resentment at him whenever I put him in her arms to be fed.

"Are you gonna drive me back to civilization when you're finished milking me like a cow?" she asked sullenly.

"I can't. I'm not headed that way."

"Well, how am I supposed to get back home?"

"You can take a bus. I'll drive you to the station."

"And when is that gonna be?"

"Like I said, four or five days. No more than a week."

"Walter's gonna start wondering where I am if he doesn't hear from me soon. Man, he's gonna be so pissed when he finds out I don't have the baby."

"Am I supposed to care about that child peddler's feelings? That man's a criminal and he belongs in jail."

"As far as the law goes, he didn't commit a crime, but you did," Ava shot back. "A double kidnapping could get you a lot of time in the clink." She shook her head gloomily. "Frankly, you should be more worried about Walter than the cops. He might resort to violence when he finds out that the baby's gone."

"He'll have to find me first...and that won't be easy."

"In that case, he might take it out on me," she said solemnly.

"That's not my problem. But if you're worried about him, then don't go back to your apartment."

"Where else am I going to go? I don't have any family to turn to. And I don't have any money to skip town. You said you were gonna pay me." She gnawed on her bottom lip, waiting for me to say something, but I didn't open my mouth. "Listen, Claire," she continued. "I don't expect the full thirty that you promised, but can't you let me have, like, ten thousand?"

"I could, but if I paid you, I wouldn't be any better than the other lawless people who perpetuate child trafficking."

"The people who're waiting to get the baby aren't criminals. They're a really nice couple. College educated. With good jobs."

"Nice people wouldn't purchase a baby; they'd go through the proper channels. This child is my flesh and blood and I'll do everything in my power to protect him from scum like Walter... and you!"

Ava rolled her eyes and returned her attention to the movie.

By midnight my eyes were getting heavy, but I fought sleep, waiting for Ava to doze off. Locking her in the bathroom was no longer an option. For one thing, I couldn't rely on the flimsy lock to keep her barricaded while I slept. Secondly, merely *thinking* about confining her inside the bathroom was totally different from actually doing it. Bringing her meals and handing over the baby to be breastfed inside the bathroom seemed utterly ridiculous in reality.

She wasn't getting out the front door without the key and the windows were all sealed shut, so I didn't have to worry about her crawling out of one of them. I could have offered her Brandon's room to rest in, but the very idea of *her* of all people luxuriating in my son's bed didn't sit well with me.

It served her right to have to try to get comfortable on the couch.

Chapter 23

Snoring loudly, Ava finally fell into a deep sleep. I crept out of the main room, carrying Bran inside the bureau drawer. I took him into my room and placed the makeshift crib on one side of my bed. I pulled back the covers on the other side and crawled in with my clothes on and my arms wrapped securely around my handbag.

I told myself I would only rest for a half-hour or so, and then I'd call my job and leave a voicemail. I was much more comfortable reciting a fabricated story of dire illness to a machine than speaking with an actual person in the Human Resources department.

I closed my eyes briefly and then for no apparent reason, I sprang upright in alarm. My head swiveled from side to side checking to see if someone had entered the room. I crept to the living room and was satisfied that Ava was still curled on the couch, sound asleep.

Back in my room, I checked the baby, making sure he was dry, and most importantly, making sure he was still breathing. Seeing his little chest rise and fall filled me with relief and I got back in bed and turned on my side with a sense of peace.

But in the next instant, my peace was shattered. The bedroom door burst open, banging loudly into the wall. Instinctually, I jumped to my feet, but couldn't get my bearing. I saw a flash of blue and white hurtling toward me and my arm went up defensively, but I was unable to protect myself from the tremendous blow that landed on the side of my head.

Bran! I thought as my world turned completely black.

I went to a timeless, shadowy place where someone was moaning, scratching, and clawing to get out. That tortured soul kept whimpering and crying and repeating the same indistinct syllable over and over again. In the background, a siren sounded.

"Braa, Braa, Braa," I muttered as I returned to consciousness and realized the tortured soul from the dark place had been me.

On the floor beside me was the brass fireplace shovel. The blare of the security alarm was deafening, undeniable proof that Ava had escaped.

What about the baby?

Oh, God, please...no...no...no!

I picked myself up and nearly fainted at the sight of the empty bureau drawer. In a state of confusion and disbelief, I inched my way over to the empty drawer, blinking rapidly as if trying to will the reappearance of my grandchild. But he was gone. Standing on wobbly legs, I cried out as I ran my hand over the woolen blanket that Bran had lain upon.

With the singular thought of getting him back, I staggered to the living room. The door was wide open and the shrill sound of the alarm was replaced by a human voice coming over the intercom. It was someone from the security company, asking repeatedly if everything was okay. I didn't bother to answer.

I stood in the doorway immune to the wind and chill as I looked out into the darkness, stunned to discover that my car was gone. I closed the door and hobbled back to the bedroom in search of my handbag.

Frantically, I ripped back the cover and the sheet, but of course, it wasn't there.

Ava had taken everything. My car, identification, money, and credit cards...and my grandson.

Tears streamed as I envisioned Bran. So tiny and helpless, and at the mercy of a lunatic who was hell-bent on selling him.

Head in my hands, slumped on the couch and sobbing, I suddenly jumped to my feet when I heard tires crunching along the dirt road. I ran to the door. Ava had had second thoughts and had brought Bran back to me. I swung the door open, laughing and grinning almost manically.

But my smile froze and then dropped when I saw the flashing lights of a state trooper's squad car. A male officer emerged from the car, shining a flashlight as he strode down the icy path with confident footfalls that seemed immune to slipping on ice.

"Is everything okay, ma'am? We received a call from your security company. They tried to reach you by phone and over the intercom and were unable to make contact."

I should have felt grateful for police assistance, but my story was so complicated and seemed so convoluted, I didn't know where to begin. I took a deep breath. "My grandson has been kidnapped," I said, wringing my hands.

"Excuse me?"

"My grandson...my car...and my purse...stolen."

He immediately called for backup. "My name is Officer Snyder. Can I come inside, ma'am?"

I stepped aside and allowed the officer entry.

He tilted his head and squinted at my head. "You have a head wound. Were you assaulted during the break-in?"

I gingerly touched the area he was referring to. My fingertips sank into a small pool of warm, gooey blood. "It wasn't a break-in."

"Was the child a boy or girl?"

"A boy."

"How old and what was he wearing?"

"He's a newborn. He was wrapped in a green blanket and was only wearing a diaper."

"And did you get a look at the perpetrator?"

"Yes, it was his mother."

"A newborn was stolen by its mother...and she fled in your car?" His eyes narrowed skeptically, like my story suddenly didn't add up. "What's the mother's name?"

I gave him Ava's full name, spelling out her last name, which he jotted down.

"Make, model, and color of the vehicle. And I need the plate number."

"It's a white Toyota Camry, but I don't know the plate number by heart. The registration card with that information is in the glove box," I explained.

"That's not a problem. I can look it up."

He spoke into the two-way radio, again, reciting Ava's full name and referring to her as the perpetrator. He named me as the victim, and gave a description of my car.

When I heard the words "assault," "robbery," "domestic dispute" and "*possible* kidnapping," the ordeal became so unbelievable and surreal, I had to take a seat on the couch.

"Okay, ma'am, I looked up your registration and put out an APB on your car. With the icy roads, your daughter wouldn't have gotten very far."

"She's not my daughter."

"I thought—"

"My son's the baby's father and—"

"I need to contact your son. Did he have custody?"

"No, he's deceased," I whimpered and tears began to seep from my eyes. At that point, I realized how insane my story sounded, but the wound on my head was proof that I'd been the victim of violence. I stood up, feeling the need to further prove my claim that the baby had been kidnapped. "I'll show you where the baby was sleeping," I said and beckoned for him to follow me to the bedroom.

We entered the room and I pointed to the fireplace shovel on the floor. "That's what she hit me with. The baby was sleeping peacefully... in there." I pointed to the empty dresser drawer and the cop visibly flinched. "I didn't have a chance to get him a crib yet," I explained.

"What's the date of birth of the infant?"

"Uh, today...I think. I mean, yesterday, maybe. Yeah, he was born before midnight."

"What hospital?"

I shook my head. "She went into labor in my car." I realized that my story was getting crazier by the minute, but I wanted the officer to have all the facts.

"Did you take the mother and infant to the hospital after the birth?"

"No."

"Why not, ma'am?"

"I couldn't. She was going to sell him on the black market and I had to keep my grandson safe from the people involved in the baby-selling ring."

"I see." He arched a brow dubiously and then closed his notepad. "Why don't we go back to the front room and wait for backup to get here."

Flashing red and blue lights announced the arrival of two local police cruisers. A team of officers came in. Two of them were carrying finger-printing kits and immediately went to work, dusting surfaces around the cabin with a dark powder.

A female officer introduced herself as Detective Graham and she ushered me to the bedroom where we could speak in private.

"Can you tell me what happened?" she asked. She had kind eyes that instantly put me at ease.

I repeated everything I'd told Officer Snyder, but feeling more comfortable, I went into more detail. Divulging how Ava had used Brandon for his sperm for the purpose of deliberately bringing a child into the world to be put up for sale.

The detective nodded, encouraging me to go on. I wept as I told her about Brandon's suicide and the awful texts I found on his phone from Ava, calling him names and goading him into shooting himself. "What she did to my son is a crime in itself," I sobbed.

I admitted to refusing to get Ava medical attention and to bringing her to the cabin against her will. "But I did it to protect the baby," I clarified. Like an idiot, I blathered on and on, often repeating myself when the detective didn't nod or murmur a sound of understanding. She merely listened without commiserating.

Finally, she said, "Ms. Wilkins. We found your car. Ava Stephenson was driving along Interstate 80 with a male infant lying across her lap."

"Oh, thank God! Where's my grandson? Is he all right?"

"He's getting checked out at the hospital as we speak."

"Please take me to him; I have to see him right away. And what about Ava...is she in police custody?"

"They're both at the hospital, ma'am. Ava is being questioned and so far, your stories match...somewhat."

"Somewhat?" I scoffed. "I'm sure she left out the part about her plan to sell her own baby."

"I'm not sure. What I do know is that you both agree that she was forced at gunpoint—"

"It was a Taser—not a real gun."

The detective continued. "She was coerced by threat of force to give birth in a car, denied medical attention, and held against her will in this cabin. Is that what happened?"

"Yes, but it's not the whole story."

The detective's face hardened. "Claire Wilkins, you're under arrest."

My knees buckled and the room seemed to spin around. "But... but...she assaulted me," I protested, touching my head injury.

Detective Graham maintained her steely look as she began reading me my rights.

In a state of shock and feeling as if I were in an alternate universe, I meekly put my hands behind my back. Without protest, I submitted to the tight, cold handcuffs that clenched my wrists.

Chapter 24

They kept me in lockup overnight and into the next day. Finally, I was arraigned and when I was led into the courtroom, it seemed that I was in some sort of warped, parallel universe.

Feeling mortified, I stood before the judge. I was so embarrassed, I couldn't bring myself to glance over at Jeff, whom I'd contacted when I was granted a phone call. There was no one else to call. Certainly not Veronica—not with her association with Walter.

Jeff had arranged everything. He'd hired a lawyer and with my car impounded, he'd made the long trip to the mountains to lend moral support and to drive me home.

During the arraignment, I was hit with a litany of charges: kidnapping, false imprisonment, aggravated assault, fetal abuse, child abduction, and child endangerment. The fetal abuse charge was due to my refusal to get Ava medical help while in labor and during childbirth.

I was considered a flight risk and the overzealous prosecutor had asked that the bail be set ridiculously high. My lawyer—God bless the man—argued on my behalf and the bail was reduced to a reasonable amount.

Retrieving my handbag, which contained my wallet, identification, and the keys to my home was a lengthy process. Jeff and I had to wait for over two hours. The Taser was kept for evidence, along with my cell phone and my car.

Afterward, I walked trancelike to Jeff's car, looking neither left nor right at the spattering of people who stood in the freezing cold outside the courthouse, curious to get a look at the crazy lady who'd kidnapped a premature infant, refused it medical care, and had held the child and its mother captive in a remote cabin.

"Wanna stop and get something to eat?" Jeff asked.

I shook my head. "I just want to get home." Food was the last thing on my mind. The act of eating had lost its appeal months ago...after Brandon died. And it had even less appeal now.

Jeff looked more handsome than I remembered. As he drove, I stole glances, unable to bring myself to look at him openly. My situation was so humiliating, I couldn't bear to look him directly in the eyes. Furthermore, I was sure I looked like death warmed over. I was tempted to pull the visor down and take a peek in the mirror, but was terrified of seeing the mask of horror that would stare back at me.

I couldn't wait to get out of the wrinkled, smelly clothes I had on. I desperately wanted to take a bath and have a long, private cry.

"Do you want to talk about it?" he asked in a gentle voice. "You're facing some serious charges. None of this is like you at all, Claire. What happened—why'd you do it?"

I wasn't ready to tell my side of the story, but I couldn't stay clammed up forever. Jeff had been waiting patiently for me get over the grieving process, and now that I was facing lengthy jail time, he deserved an explanation.

"I don't know where to begin."

"Begin with the flight back from Paris. That's when you began putting up a wall...and that was the last time I saw you."

"Right. I couldn't get in touch with Brandon and I was scared out of my mind. When I confided in you about his problems, I didn't tell you the whole story. I left out the fact that he had set up housekeeping with a mean, psycho girl named Ava and her lesbian lover, Muffy."

"Huh? What?" Jeff whipped his head in my direction and then quickly returned his eyes to the road.

"Exactly. The way Brandon was living was too raunchy for me to speak of."

"Hearing that your son lived with a lesbian couple took me off guard, but I didn't mean to seem judgmental. People should be able to live and love the way they choose."

"But Ava didn't love him. She was using him to get pregnant. She tricked him into believing she wanted to start a family with him, but all she really wanted was to make money by selling the child."

Jeff shot me a look of incredulity.

"Yes," I said emphatically. "Ava is a conniving, money-hungry liar—a real piece of work. Brandon wasn't perfect by any means, but he was innocent compared to that con artist. You wouldn't believe how ruthless and cruel she could be. Brandon had such self-loathing, he allowed her to demean him and he agreed to share her with a woman because he didn't want to lose her.

"My actions probably seem drastic. I'm sure what I did seems insane, but I did it for the love for my grandchild. To protect him from a fate no child deserves."

Jeff reached over and caressed my hand. "During our short relationship, you never talked much about your past. You didn't say much about your son or your ex-husband, and I didn't pry. But I want to know your story, Claire." He paused and I noticed his Adam's apple bob as he contemplated what to say next. "I want to help you get out of this mess because I love you, Claire."

When he said he loved me, I became a crying, blubbery mess. I felt so undeserving.

"I never gave up on us, but if there's even a prayer for us to repair our relationship, you have to stop being so secretive. There has to be trust between us from now on. I need to understand you and know who you really are."

No man had ever spoken to me so lovingly or treated me with such human compassion. Jeff's gentle kindness prompted me to cry even harder.

"Hey, hey, it's gonna be okay," he said softly, rubbing my shoulder with his free hand. "Tell me about Brandon...about the relationship between you two."

Sniveling, wiping my eyes and my nose, I began talking about my son. Beginning with when he was a cuddly, happy baby.

I told him Brandon's entire heartbreaking story. How I'd been partly responsible for not standing up for him when Howard treated him with such contempt. How I'd tried to make up for my negligence after the divorce, but it had been too late. And how I'd condoned his outbursts and downright rudeness when he grew older out of a sense of guilt.

My tears had dried by the time I got to the part about bumping into Ava at Home Depot, but when I reached the part of the story where I discovered the empty dresser drawer, the tears began to fall in torrents, all over again.

"I'm so worried about little Bran," I sobbed.

"He's in good hands at the hospital," Jeff assured me. "And now that the court's involved, she can't wantonly sell the child to the highest bidder; she'll have to account for the child's whereabouts."

"What about the man, Walter Caulfield? Suppose he overpowers Ava and takes the baby right out of her arms? I get the impression that he's not kidding around."

"With the media attention surrounding this case, I can guarantee you that anyone involved in an illegal baby-selling ring has already skipped town."

"Do you really think so?"

"If he's in his right mind, he took the loss and got the hell out of Middletown. Listen, Claire, instead of speculating, why don't you get his home address from your friend, and I'll pay him a visit."

"No, Jeff. I don't want you to get involved with him. He's a dangerous man."

Jeff scoffed. "He's a coward and a bully that preys on impoverished young women. Let's see how he stands up to me."

"No, you've helped me enough. I don't want you getting mixed up in this mess."

"If you feel threatened by this Walter guy, then I'm already involved."

In another lifetime, I would have been swooning over Jeff's open admission of his feelings for me, but under the circumstances, with my freedom being threatened and my fear of what the future held for Bran, all I could do was wring my hands.

"Even if Walter went away, the baby's life is still in jeopardy if he's left with Ava. She's bad news, Jeff. She's an awful human being. No redeeming qualities. She's so completely damaged and unbearably narcissistic, I think something's missing in her. I honestly don't believe she has it in her to care about anyone other than herself."

"I hate to be the one to break the news to you, but the media is depicting her as a courageous mother and a hero who managed to escape from her cruel abductor."

"They're calling me cruel and portraying me as a monster when I was trying to save an innocent life from the real monster." I groaned loud and long. "Obviously the way I handled the situation was bizarre and outrageous. I'm sure there were better options, but when her water broke, I panicked. She wanted her phone and I was terrified she was going to call the baby brokers that had been supporting her and had promised her a lump sum upon delivery of the baby."

Jeff caressed my arm comfortingly.

We rode in silence for a while, both of us deep in thought.

"I have an idea," Jeff announced.

I glanced at him.

"Besides you, Ava is the only other person who knows the real story. She knows the truth about your motives—that you were trying to prevent her from selling your grandchild."

"Yes, but surely you don't think that a self-serving girl like her would ever admit the truth? I bet she's having a grand ol' time at the hospital, enjoying her celebrity status and putting on quite a show for the staff. Probably insisting that the baby stay close to her and pretending to fear that someone will take him from her again. I can see her now, showering him with kisses, and pretending to be the picture of selfless motherhood in front of the staff, yet I had to threaten her with violence just to get her to feed her child."

Jeff nodded his head. "Things look pretty bleak right now, I know. But my wheels are starting to spin and I may have an idea that will clear your name."

Despite Jeff's optimism, I sighed regretfully. "With Ava's testimony and the way I stupidly blurted out a confession to that female detective, I don't see how I'm going to get out of this mess, unscathed." I shook my head grimly. "I had a lot of time to think while I was locked up, and I've decided to plead insanity. I'm going to discuss it with my attorney when I meet with him tomorrow. After all, I spent thirty days in the psych ward after I lost Brandon. That should help my case; don't you think?"

"It sounds like you want to give up without a fight, and I'm not going to let you do that. I'll fight for you even if you won't fight for yourself."

Suddenly misty-eyed again, I quickly turned my head and gazed out the window.

Chapter 25

When Jeff pulled into my driveway, I was stunned to see a crowd of gawkers standing on the pavement outside my house. I hadn't expected that. Some of the onlookers were neighbors I'd known for years, and many others I'd never seen before. There was even a news van, for God's sake.

What the spectators all had in common was a collective rage that was directed at me. Glaring at me, the mob snarled and murmured scornful sounds.

I emerged from the car with my head down. I would have preferred disappearing through a hole in the ground, rather than having to face anyone.

Jeff put his arm around me and led the way. We had to push our way past the angry gawkers who soon heightened the chaos by shouting awful names. "Child Snatcher," "Baby Thief," and "Crazy Bitch" were a few choice phrases that were hurled at me.

The set of keys shook so badly in my hand, Jeff had to take them from me and unlock the front door.

Inside I collapsed into a chair. "I can't believe this is happening."

"It'll pass," Jeff soothed.

"But what about you? You didn't do anything wrong. Won't being associated with me affect your business image?"

"I doubt it. Besides, I don't care."

The landline phone began to ring. I glanced at the screen.

"Who is it?" Jeff asked.

"The number's blocked."

"Ignore it."

"It might be the attorney."

"Why would he—"

"Hello?" I said before Jeff could finish his sentence.

"I want to know one thing, Claire," Howard bellowed into the phone. "Why the hell are you still using my last name?"

"I kept your name for Brandon's sake—so we'd have the same last name. You know that."

"Well, he's dead now, so move on and start using your own fucking last name. I don't want to be associated with you in any way, you goddamn lunatic. My phones at the office won't stop ringing and they're not business calls. I'm getting harassed by reporters—I even got a call from the fucking *Daily Mail* in the UK for crying out loud. Between you and Brandon, you've both succeeded in sullying my good name. I don't understand why they didn't keep you in the nuthouse. Obviously, that's where you belong."

Hearing me gasp and seeing my face go ashen, Jeff took the phone from my hand.

"Who is it?" he demanded.

"It's my ex," I whispered in a meek voice.

"Say, Bud...I doubt that this is a social call, so if you're trying to add to Claire's problems, I suggest you leave her alone and get a life. Otherwise, I'll be paying you a visit. And we can deal with your gripes, man-to-man."

Jeff took the phone from his ear and stared at it. "He hung up.

What a punk!" He turned his gaze on me. "Listen, Claire. You're probably going to get a lot more calls from blocked numbers, and I suggest you ignore them unless you enjoy listening to a bunch of crap."

"You're right. I'll stop answering it."

"In fact, unplug the phone right now."

"But what about—"

"Don't worry about the attorney being able to contact you. I'm going to go out and get you a new cell phone, and no one gets the number except the attorney and me."

"Okay."

"Meanwhile, try to relax until I get back."

I nodded and Jeff kissed me on the forehead and then whisked out the door.

Surrounded by familiar things, I wandered from room to room with a vague sense of contentment. It was good to be home, but I couldn't fully enjoy it with a mob surrounding my house. The buzz of their angry voices carried to the inside and I wasn't able to shut out the sound until I went upstairs into the bathroom and turned the faucet on, full force.

As the bathtub filled, I meandered into my bedroom and glimpsed my laptop on the desk. I was tempted to go online and read about Ava's abduction, but I decided against it. Reading a bunch of lies about myself would not improve my emotional status.

I accidentally glimpsed my image in a full-length mirror that stood in a corner of my room. I cringed at the sight of me. My face was flushed. My eyes were red-rimmed and watery. I looked like an un-bathed street person with oily, stringy hair and disheveled clothing.

I tore off my clothes with the intention of throwing them in the trash or better yet, burning them. But in the meantime, I stuck them in the clothes hamper, pushing them to the bottom.

In the bathroom, I sank down into the tub of hot water. But instead of feeling better, I immediately began worrying about Bran. Was he doing all right? The doctor had surely separated him from the placenta by now and had put him on baby formula.

Despite the stellar performance Ava was giving as she pretended to be a loving mother, I doubted if she'd willingly continue to breast-feed. But at least my little guy was getting good medical care. That was the only upside to this tragic story.

Oh, Bran. What's going to happen to you when Ava takes you home and the public has turned their attention to the next salacious story?

Being immersed in water soothed me. I soaked for so long, my body had shriveled like a prune.

A sudden pounding on the front door startled me and I rose from the water with a great splash. Donning a white robe and slippers and with a towel tied around my head, I padded down the stairs and cautiously peeked through the curtains. I expected to see Jeff, but to my utter surprise, Veronica was standing on my porch, and she was being jeered by the crowd.

I threw the locks off and yanked the door open. She burst inside and embraced me in a bear hug. "Claire. Oh, my God. How are you doing?"

"I've been better."

"What possessed you to abduct that young woman and her child?"

I disengaged from Veronica's embrace and looked her in the eyes. "That child is my grandson. He's Brandon's child."

"What!" Veronica looked shocked.

"And the mother, that rotten bitch, Ava Stephenson, intended to sell him..." I paused. "To a child-selling ring. And Walter Caulfield is involved."

Veronica recoiled.

"I know you believe that Walter is a good guy, but he's not. He's the quintessential wolf in sheep's clothing. I don't expect you to believe me, but some way, somehow, the truth will eventually come out."

"I believe you, Claire," she said in a hushed voice.

"Really? You believe me?" I was stunned.

She nodded. "You know that saying, there's no fool like an old fool. Well, Walter really had me duped."

"I need his address, Veronica. To give to the police."

"It won't do you any good," she said gravely.

"What do you mean? Why not?"

"He skipped town the minute the story about that girl hit the news." Veronica covered her face with her hands. "And I'm ashamed to say, he absconded with my life's savings. All the money my hardworking, sweet Freddie left me, as well as my own savings. It's all gone."

"How'd that happen?" I couldn't keep the outrage out of my voice.

"He scammed me, Claire. Tricked me into some kind of offshore investing. Claimed I could get a big break in taxes and triple my money." Veronica let out a sharp cry. "Oh, I'm so ashamed of myself— for being so stupid. Now he's gone, and so is my retirement fund."

"Are you sure?"

She nodded. "His house has been cleared out completely. Walter's in the wind. I've seen stories on TV about foolish widows like myself, but they usually get deceived by handsome young studs. Not a seemingly kindly senior citizen who bird watches and volunteers at the city zoo. I'm five years older than Walter, but that's not a big age difference."

"Being a volunteer was a good cover," I said grimly.

"Yeah, Walter was a crafty ol' son-of-a-gun," Veronica bitterly admitted.

Trying to comfort her, I patted her hand. "Did you go to the police?"

"Not yet. This is a small town and news travels. I don't want the whole town gossiping about my stupidity before I talk with my children."

I nodded in understanding.

"Enough about me; I came to lend you my support. I knew you

couldn't have done the malicious things they're saying you did, unless you'd gone completely off your rocker. I can't tell you how good it is to see that you didn't go crazy, again. Oh, goodness, I didn't mean that to come out the way it did."

"It's okay," I assured her.

"So, what are you going to do?"

"I don't know. My friend Jeff has a plan."

"Who's Jeff?"

"Remember the guy we saw rock climbing at the community center? The handsome one with the silver hair?"

"The Richard Gere look-alike?"

I nodded and gave a faint smile. "We were secretly dating. We went to Paris when I took that spur-of-the-moment vacation."

Veronica hooted in laughter. "You sly ol' fox. I never suspected a thing!"

"But when we got back and after everything happened with Brandon, I broke it off. Anyway, he has a plan that might get me less time...maybe get me off completely." I shrugged and smiled sadly. "I don't know. We'll see what happens."

Chapter 26

Jeff didn't return to my house with a new phone until the next day. His face held a bleak expression and I could tell that he had bad news to deliver.

"What's wrong?" I asked, though I dreaded his answer.

"I visited Ava at the hospital."

"Why?"

"To make a deal with her."

"What sort of deal?"

"You stated that she'd only gone through with the pregnancy to make money, but being under public scrutiny, she couldn't go through with her plan."

"That's right..." I waited for him to continue.

"I offered her a large sum of money if she'd recant her statement and tell the public why you were so desperate to get your grandson away from her. I told her that she'd probably be charged with making fraudulent statements and for filing a false police report, but she'd most likely spend less than a year in prison or she'd possibly get off on probation. I assured her that the money would be put in safe-keeping for her if she granted you custody of your grandson."

"What did she say?" I asked anxiously.

Jeff ran a hand through his hair. "No deal. I was so sure she'd go for it, but she wouldn't. She said she had a plan of her own that would bring in big bucks. I left my card with her, in case she has a change of heart."

Later that day, Jeff accompanied me to the lawyer's office, and we all agreed that my best bet was an insanity plea.

While I was being maligned and vilified by the press, there was an outpour of sympathy for Ava. Opportunist that she was, she set up a GoFundMe account, and raised over $15,000 in a single day. People from all over the world were contributing and it appeared that Ava would make a much larger profit from online donations than Walter's organization had offered her. Manufacturers had gotten in on the bandwagon, pledging donations of disposable diapers, baby furniture, baby food, and infant wear.

After three days, Ava was medically cleared to leave the hospital, but the baby was kept for further observation. A nearby hotel kindly provided Ava with free lodging until her child was released.

For a girl like Ava who'd spent her childhood being shuffled from one foster home to the next, all the attention she'd been receiving was a cause for celebration.

And the celebrating got out of hand.

According to news reports, guests at the hotel had complained repeatedly about the amount of noise emanating from Ava's room and were leery of the stream of unsavory characters that drifted in and out of her room.

When she neglected to visit the baby at the hospital for days in a row, hospital staff, unable to reach her by phone, alerted hotel management and asked them to check on her.

What they discovered was a practically comatose Ava, sprawled out, half-naked on the bed. And there was a host of unidentified men and women in various stages of undress, passed out on the floor and slumped in chairs.

There was also a plethora of alcohol, but the police were alerted when the hotel staff discovered a large quantity of drugs. The police seized a half-pound of methamphetamine, a pound of marijuana, and a half-pound of cocaine.

The group of partiers was taken to the hospital and from there they were carted off to jail. They all pointed the finger at Ava, claiming she had bought the drugs with her GoFundMe windfall and had plans to distribute them.

Seemingly overnight, Ava went from courageous survivor and mother-of-the-year to a reviled criminal being dubbed, "Monster Mom."

Donations that were intended to help give her child a good start in life had been used to fund wild sex parties and to pay for large quantities of drugs.

The public was outraged.

A hotshot female attorney took Ava's case pro bono. In the hope of garnering sympathy for Ava, the attorney held a press conference and vividly described the abuse that Ava suffered at the hands of numerous foster parents during her tough childhood.

Shockingly, Ava did have a smidgeon of humanity in her. She told the authorities that she'd lied on me and that she wanted to drop all the charges.

Taking advantage of our sudden turn of good fortune, my lawyer claimed that the knock upside my head should have been treated before I was questioned and that while suffering a concussion, I had agreed to a crime I'd never committed. My attorney spun a convincing tale. According to him, Ava had gone into labor while we were on our way to the mountains for a short vacation. Neither of us had expected her to go into labor at seven months.

He further claimed that I had taken her to the cabin instead of the hospital because Ava had insisted on a home birth from the very beginning of her pregnancy.

Ava corroborated my attorney's claims.

In the aftermath of being exonerated, neighbors, wearing sheepish expressions, stopped by with offerings of fruit baskets, casseroles, cakes, and pies.

But nothing made me happier than the day Ava called Jeff from prison wanting to accept the deal he'd previously offered. Crafty girl that she was, she spoke in code in case the call was being monitored.

Although I was staunchly opposed to treating children as a commodity, I knew without a shadow of a doubt that Ava was a horrible mother and would find a way to make money off Bran one way or another if she was ever given the opportunity.

She was sentenced to eight years in prison, and would probably be out in five or less with good behavior. The way the foster care system worked, when she was released, she'd be eligible to get Bran back if she completed parenting classes and could accommodate him with suitable housing.

With the foster care system overloaded with cases, it wasn't likely that anyone would monitor Ava for very long.

She was a damaged woman and I didn't believe that any amount of therapy or rehabilitation would ever change who she was. Even if she decided against selling Bran to the highest bidder and chose to raise him herself, I doubted he'd ever be safe with her.

And so, I made a secret, verbal agreement to set aside a certain amount of money that would be available to Ava when she was released. She, in turn, would not challenge my petition to adopt Bran.

As a family member, it was relatively easy for me to be awarded temporary custody of my grandson. With Ava's cooperation, a legal adoption was in the works, but it would take up to a year to be finalized.

Meanwhile, having little Bran in my life made me the happiest woman in the world.

Jeff and I were closer than ever and very much in love. We both agreed that marriage was an outdated institution and neither of us required a piece of paper as proof of our commitment to each other.

After being swindled out of her entire retirement savings, Veronica notified the FBI and discovered that Walter Caulfield aka Lester Pennington had been on their radar for many years for a number of crimes including money laundering, bribery, and embezzlement. There was nothing that linked him to any black market baby rings, but that wasn't surprising since the majority of child traffickers operated clandestinely.

It wasn't easy for Veronica to rebuild. She continued working at the zoo and she earned extra income employed as a part-time nanny for Bran.

With a small fortune in the bank, I could afford to stay home and be a full-time mom to Bran. During the winter months, we spent a great deal of time indoors and I always looked forward to date night with Jeff. Jeff was my hero. My modern-day knight in shining armor.

Although the neighbors that had known me for years seemed satisfied that I was innocent, mistrust lingered among the people who only knew me in passing. I was still very much the source of gossip in Middletown. At the supermarket, movie theater, or local swap meet, I often caught glimpses of people whispering about me behind their hands.

Occasionally when pushing Bran in his stroller, I'd hear murmurings: "Is that the child she stole from its mother?" I can't say that the cruelty of others didn't hurt because it did.

Jeff suggested we relocate. Somewhere far away—where I wasn't known. He was also concerned that Bran would be affected by the gossip when he got older, but that was something we'd have to deal with at a later time.

I couldn't leave Middletown until after the adoption was finalized, and so I conditioned myself to ignore the whispers and gossip. I was so grateful to have a good man who loved me and a beautiful grandson who was the center of my universe.

I couldn't bear to think about what would have become of me had it not been for Jeff sticking by my side throughout one of the worst ordeals of my life.

Chapter 27

O n Bran's first birthday, we had several reasons to celebrate. I had officially become his adopted mother and on the day before his birthday, Bran had taken his first steps, which Jeff recorded.

We threw him a birthday party in town at the Please Touch Museum. Watching the playful yet tender way Jeff interacted with Bran touched me deeply, and put tears in my eyes. If only Brandon's father had treated him with such love and kindness, maybe my son would still be with me today. As misguided as Brandon was, he seemed clear about wanting a child. I think in his own quirky way, he thought bringing a child into the world would redeem him.

Jeff was in the midst of helping Bran explore a giant dump truck, and I was supposed to be filming the moment, but the hand that held the camera dropped listlessly to my side.

When Jeff noticed me wiping tears from my eyes, he took Bran out of the dump truck and strode over to me.

"What's going on?" he inquired.

"I'm having a moment, but I'll be okay." I tried to chuckle but couldn't quite manage it, and the sound that emerged sounded like the cry of a suffering animal.

"Are those tears of joy or is something else happening?"

"A little of both—I'm ecstatic that Bran is happy and healthy and that I have you in my life, but I miss Brandon so much and I wish he could experience this moment with his son. With Bran in his life, I think my son would have finally found the happiness that eluded him." I made a squeaky sound as I tried to stifle a sob.

Jeff embraced me. "It's okay, babe. It's okay," he said soothingly as I sobbed against his chest.

A few weeks after Bran's first birthday I took him to a photographer for professional pictures. I loved capturing the many physical changes that had occurred since his infancy. His hair had been dark and curly like Brandon's during his first few months, but somewhere along the way, his hair had become straight with a reddish hue. With his super long lashes, he was the most beautiful child I'd ever seen. He still had Brandon's eyes and nose and I was grateful that none of Ava's physical characteristics were visible in him.

The photographer, who spoke with an Irish lilt, set Bran up with a beach ball, bucket and shovel, and placed him on a blanket, creating a beach scene. Bran was such an agreeable baby, it was easy to get him to smile and laugh.

Midway into the photo shoot, the photographer, assuming that I was Bran's natural mother, asked me if the Irish blood he saw in Bran was from my side of the family or his father's.

"Neither," I responded. I didn't know anything about Ava's ancestry and wasn't interested in knowing. As far as Howard and I were concerned, there wasn't a drop of Irish in either of us.

"Oh, I thought this little redhead was a sturdy Irish lad. I must be getting old." The photographer chuckled to himself and began gathering stuffed animals that would be used as background props for the next shoot.

Although I tried to laugh it off, a deeper part of me was troubled. So much so that when I got home, I ordered a DNA kit online. When the kit arrived, I swabbed the inside of Bran's cheeks and my own as per the instructions of the grandparentage test.

I was on pins and needles during the days that led up to receiving the results. When they finally arrived in an email, I anxiously opened it. I peered at the information through squinted eyes that quickly widened. My eyes raced over the wording and scanned the numbers at least ten times before I covered my mouth with my hand and slumped in the chair.

My eyes traveled from the computer screen over to Bran who was sitting on the floor playing with a toy car. I gazed at him in disbelief and then released a tiny whimper.

My emotions were all over the place. I felt like I was having an out-of-body experience. It didn't seem real. But the facts were facts. If fifty percent of Bran's DNA had come from Brandon, there should have been twenty-five percent from me, yet the results stated that Bran and I shared zero percent DNA.

That goddamn Ava was such a corrupt human being and a monstrous liar! My lips parted wide and I cried out in anguish. My baby...my little Bran was no relation to me.

Back when I had bumped into Ava at Home Depot, I'd made the assumption that she was pregnant with Brandon's child and she strung me along for the ride.

All this time, I'd treated Ava decently. Kept money on her books, sent her photos of Bran, and had even contemplated taking him to the prison for a visit.

It was no wonder that my son had been so easily manipulated by Ava. She was the master of manipulation and my son and I had both been fools.

Devastated, I wept into my hands.

I sat in the crowded, noisy visitor's room waiting for Ava to be brought out. When she spotted me, she waved and broke into a huge grin—like we were long-lost friends.

"Hi, Claire," she said cheerfully. "I don't get many visitors—Muffy comes every now and then, but she has a new girl, now." She prattled on for a few more moments and then noticed that Bran wasn't with me. "Hey, I thought you were going to bring the baby with you."

"Prison isn't the kind of place I want my son to become familiar with," I said coldly.

Noticing my tone, she looked at me skeptically. "Why do you have a bug up your ass?"

I glared at her. "This isn't a social visit. I only came to let you know that we're moving."

A surprised look crossed her face. "Really? Where're you going? Nowhere too far, I hope. We agreed that I could be a part of Bran's life when I get out."

"No, I don't think so. I've changed my mind."

She leaned forward and laughed nervously. "I hope you didn't change your mind about that other arrangement we agreed on. I'm looking forward to that nest egg you put aside for me," she said in a confidential tone.

"I've changed my mind about that too," I replied, looking her square in the eyes.

"You're fucking kidding, right?"

"I'm dead serious."

"You can't do that. I gave you my fucking kid."

"No, you tried to *sell* me your fucking kid."

"I don't recall you being all holier than thou when you accepted the offer."

"He's mine now—legally adopted. You don't have any more leverage."

"You bitch," she spat in a low tone. "I lied for you and took the full blame when your crazy ass could have killed both me and your grandchild when you denied us medical care."

I leaned forward and spoke softly. "First of all, Bran is not my grandchild, so cut the crap."

Ava took on the appearance of a cornered animal as she glanced around the room. I half expected her to call for a guard, but she didn't. Her face hardened. "If someone's stupid enough to buy me shit and offer me money, I'd be a fool to turn it down."

"You're scum. And I'm glad to be rid of you once and for all. I only stopped by to let you know that there'll be no more money on your books. No more shopping sprees at the commissary," I said tauntingly.

"Fuck you and your money. I'm not worried. Another sucker is bound to come along." She leered at me and propped her elbow on the back of the chair, pleased with herself. "And another thing, don't think you can get rid of me that easily. I'm all in that kid's bloodstream. If he doesn't take after me, then he's bound to take after his daddy. And his daddy is a bigger con artist than me."

My pulse rate sped up and I felt faint. From what I'd read about nature versus nurture, rearing a child in a good home didn't necessarily override the child's innate behavioral traits that were embedded in his DNA. Learning that both Bran's parents were corrupt and immoral people left me badly shaken and I wondered what kind of child I was raising.

"Do you know who the father is?" I asked shakily.

"Hell, yeah, I know who the father is. Bran's daddy is Walter Caulfield."

My heart skipped several beats. "Walter Caulfield?"

"Yep," Ava said proudly.

Please God, no. Hadn't I suffered enough? Please let this be a cruel joke. My baby could not have been fathered by a master criminal that the FBI couldn't catch. And with a mother that was the scum of the earth, was it possible that my child would have an ounce of decency?

Enjoying my reaction, Ava elaborated, wearing a cruel smile. "Yeah, ol' Walter got spooked when I got popped, but I'm surprised that he hasn't come back to claim his seed. It's a good thing you're skipping town, Claire. You get to buy yourself a little time. Because if I know Walter like I think I do, he won't give up easily. He'll track you down and find you, eventually."

Ava sneered at me. "Guard!" she bellowed. When the guard appeared at our table, she stood up. "This visit is over. Take me back to my cage."

Epilogue

I'd never told Jeff about the DNA test or my discovery about Walter. I didn't give him any explanation for why I kept moving. Every six months or so, I'd think I saw Walter in the midst of a crowd at an amusement park. Or in line behind me at the ATM machine. It was beyond nerve-racking. I was terrified that he'd steal Bran and sell him to a child pornographer or any of the numerous predators that preyed on children.

After the first year of running and not explaining why, Jeff had had enough. I couldn't blame him. It was difficult for him to conduct his business never knowing when I was going to start throwing our possessions in storage bins and boxes. Maybe if I'd been brave enough to share the truth with him, he would have stuck it out with me. But I was too ashamed to admit that I'd been duped into believing that Bran was my grandchild. I wasn't sure if Jeff would still love him if he knew the truth.

Now it was only Bran and me, living in a small town in Wyoming. So far, so good. I felt safe. No shadowy figures in the crowd, watching me from afar.

I discovered that love is love. Bran's genetic makeup didn't change the way I felt about him. I loved him every bit as much as I had loved my own son. And I would protect him with my life.

It was obvious to me that his genetics had no bearing on his character. He was nothing like his biological parents. I had molded and shaped him into a fine little boy who was intelligent, kind, and had principles. Even at the tender age of five he exhibited personality traits that made me proud.

I was afraid for Bran to be out of my sight for an entire day, and so I homeschooled him. Learning came so easily to him that he often finished his schoolwork between noon and one p.m. Most days, we'd go on an outing after he'd completed his lessons. To the park, a museum, and sometimes we'd take a tour bus ride to become familiar with our new city.

Bran had an abundance of toys. Practically everything on the market, but he didn't get to interact much with other kids, and that saddened me.

I was thrilled that a neighbor down the street had a little boy Bran's age. His name was Ryan and he was a delightful child. Polite like Bran and even-tempered. Last week they'd had a playdate and were scheduled for another visit today.

We arrived at the appointed hour and I lifted Bran up so he could ring the doorbell. I lowered him down to the porch when Ryan's mom opened the door. I could tell right away that she was upset about something, but I didn't appreciate the way she was glowering at Bran.

"What is it, Polly? What's wrong?"

"Your son is a thief," she exclaimed, poking her finger in Bran's direction.

"What?"

"He stole Ryan's coin collection and I ought to call the police. Ryan's coins were priceless, and he would have had them to treasure for years to come if I hadn't allowed young Bernie Madoff here to come snooping around," she ranted. "Mark my words, your boy is going to end up in the penitentiary."

"I don't understand. What are you saying?" I clutched Bran next to me and put my arm around him.

"Ryan inherited his great-grandfather's collection and it contained rare coins from all over the world. Priceless silver dollars from the eighteen-hundreds, rare quarters and dimes."

I couldn't believe this hysterical woman was accusing my innocent five-year-old of committing a crime. "Why do you think Bran took the coins?"

"Ryan showed Bran his collection the last time he was here, and then Ryan put them away before Bran left. Bran seemed to enjoy learning about the coins so much that Ryan planned to show them again, but when he took out the leather book that they're kept in, all the silver dollars, quarters and dimes were gone. Every single one of them." She twisted her lips and glared at Bran. "But your son left all the foreign currency."

"There has to be a mistake. Bran would never do anything like that. He has no reason to steal anything," I sputtered, insulted and appalled beyond belief.

"Oh, he did it all right. I'm sure of it. That little con artist might fool you, but he doesn't fool me for one darn minute. That boy of yours is as shifty as a ten-speed clutch," Polly accused.

At a loss for words, I grabbed Bran by the hand and rushed off the porch. During the walk back home, Bran asked me repeatedly why Ryan's mom was mad at him.

At first I pretended not to know, and then I turned and faced him. I got down on one knee, making myself eye level with him. "Tell me the truth, sweetheart. Mommy won't be upset.

Did you accidentally take any of Ryan's coins the last time you visited him?"

Bran furrowed his brows and shook his head. "No, Mommy. That would be stealing."

"Exactly," I agreed. "And you know that Mommy will give you everything your heart desires. You have no reason to ever steal anything from anyone...ever. Am I clear, Bran?"

Wearing a confused expression, he nodded.

I was terribly upset with Polly for accusing him of stealing. "Ryan probably misplaced his coin collection," I said to Bran as we walked along.

"Can I go over his house and play tomorrow?" Bran asked, looking up at me with his innocent eyes.

"I don't think so, honey. You'll have to find a new best friend."

"But I want Ryan to be my best friend."

"I know you do. I'm sorry, honey. But you can't have any more playdates with Ryan."

It worried me that Bran would be labeled a thief, causing other parents to be wary of him. Experiencing rejection for the first time in his life had to hurt and I wanted to take his mind off of it.

"Do you want to stop at Seven-Eleven and get a Slurpee?"

Bran's face lit up. "Yaaaay! A Slurpee!"

He was excited because I didn't typically allow him to eat a lot of sugar. But after the ordeal at Polly's, I wanted to cheer him up. As soon as we entered the store, the clerk behind the counter raised a hand, gesturing for me to stop.

"Sorry, ma'am. I can't serve you. And your little son is not allowed inside this store."

Stunned, my hand pressed against my chest. "What are you saying? Why isn't he allowed to be in here?"

"We have him on camera, ma'am. Every time you bring him in

here, he goes up and down the aisle, stuffing his pockets with candy. All the goodies are within his reach and he helps himself."

"But he's just a little kid. I'll pay whatever I owe you." Near tears, I felt desperate.

"Keep your money. Just don't bring that boy back. He's not welcome here." Glowering at us, the man pointed to the door.

I held back the tears for as long as I could, but by the time we reached our house, I was sobbing. With shaking hands, I closed and locked the front door.

"Did you take Ryan's coin collection?" I yelled at Bran, clenching his shoulders and shaking him.

"No, Mommy. I didn't."

"Why have you been stealing candy from the store?"

"I'm sorry," he said in a cracked voice, his little face scowling miserably. "I like candy, but you won't let me have it 'cause it's bad for my teeth."

"Do you think it's okay to steal something that doesn't belong to you?" I yelled.

He shook his head and started crying pitifully.

I felt so sorry for him, I pulled him into my arms and hugged him tight. I told him I was sorry for yelling.

By dinnertime, Bran was back to his normal, cheerful self. He seemed completely over the 7-Eleven trouble and had accepted that he wouldn't be invited back to Ryan's. He still hadn't admitted to taking the coins, and I held on to a glimmer of hope that stealing candy was his greatest misdeed.

But my gut told me different. I was deeply troubled and wondering what kind of child I was raising. Hadn't all the love and care I'd given him mattered at all? Or was he genetically predisposed to lie and steal? And if so, what could I do about it?

I'd schlepped Brandon to a series of psychologists and psychiatrists, and dreaded having to go down that path again. But I couldn't sit back and do nothing. Maybe if I got Bran into counseling at a young age, I could prevent him from progressing to armed robbery later in life.

On second thought, with his intelligence, he was more likely to commit cybercrimes or banking fraud. Or worse! He had a double set of criminal genes and there was no telling what kind of immoral person he was apt to become with Ava and Walter as parents.

Nevertheless, I couldn't give up on Bran. I loved him too much to believe that his future was hopeless.

At bedtime, I read him two chapters of *Harry Potter* and when he drifted off to sleep, I began searching his room, looking for Ryan's coin collection, and hoping to God I wouldn't find it.

A peculiar bulge in his oversized teddy bear caught my eye. I crept over to it and discovered a slit in the fabric in the back. I stuck my hand inside and when I pulled out a pouch that used to hold a pair of binoculars, my breath caught in my throat.

Holding the pouch, I walked trancelike out of Bran's room and into mine. I opened the pouch and shook out the contents.

Silver dollars, half-dollars, quarters, nickels, and dimes spilled out and clattered onto my bedspread. "Oh, my God," I said in a hushed whisper as I raced to the bathroom.

In front of the toilet, I dropped to my knees and vomited.

It didn't take long to finish loading up the car. In the course of the past four years, I'd learned the art of packing fast. The only difference in this move was that it was taking place in the dead of night.

Before leaving our neighborhood, I made a pit stop at Polly's house. I didn't ring the bell. I quietly placed the pouch filled with Ryan's coin collection inside the mailbox and then dashed to my car.

"Where're we going this time, Mommy?" Bran asked from the backseat.

"I was thinking Arizona, sweetie." I tried to sound cheerful, but I was terribly unhappy. Bone tired and weary.

When I'd shown Bran the stolen coins I'd found inside the stuffed animal, his reaction was troubling. Feigning astonishment, his eyes widened in delight. "Did the tooth fairy leave those for me?"

"Why would the tooth fairy leave you anything when you didn't lose a tooth?" I was amazed by his cunning and horrified by his deceitful smile.

"Maybe she left me all that money because I've been such a good little boy," he said, maintaining an expression of innocence.

Without uttering another word, I simply began tossing items into plastic crates.

After all I'd gone through to get Bran away from Ava, I couldn't turn my back on him now. We had to leave Wyoming and go somewhere where he could get a fresh start. I couldn't stay here and allow him to be labeled a thief and be ostracized by his peers.

Since discovering the stolen coins, it had briefly occurred to me to stop running and let Walter catch up with us. Let him claim his thieving son.

But I couldn't do that to Bran. It wasn't as if Walter wanted to provide a loving home for him. His only reason for pursuing us was to seize his offspring and put him on the auction block and sell him to a pedophile.

The stresses of being on the run with Bran had taken a toll on me. I glanced in the rearview mirror and cringed at my haggard reflection. It was if I were seeing the deepening lines in my face, my rapidly graying hair, and the bags under my eyes for the very first time.

"Does Arizona sound good to you, Bran?"

"I'm looking up facts about Arizona, right now," he responded, his head down as he studied the screen of his iPad. Brushing back his red hair, he looked up at me, his eyes filled with intelligence. "There's a large Native American population there. Can we visit a reservation? I want to learn about their culture," he said enthusiastically.

"Sure, we could attend a powwow or one of their ceremonies."

"Yay!" He rubbed his hands together excitedly and I was reminded of how Walter had rubbed his hands together at the idea of volunteering in the horticulture department. What Walter had actually been excited about was the possibility of finding a mark for his next big con, and he found Veronica.

The last time I'd been in touch with Veronica, I was saddened to learn she'd gotten hip replacement surgery and that it hadn't healed correctly. She was wheelchair dependent now and was residing at an assisted-living facility.

From the rearview mirror, I regarded Bran warily, wondering if he'd seen a sparkly trinket on a Native American website. Or an interesting ancient artifact that he craved to stuff inside his pocket. It was terrible having to second-guess my son's motives, but I didn't have a choice. I no longer trusted him and had to make sure I stayed several steps ahead of him.

Now that I was aware of Bran's penchant for lying and stealing, it was my responsibility as a parent to keep him on the right track. By enlisting the help of a child psychologist, hopefully Bran would be provided with tools that would teach him how to deal with his larcenous tendencies. With lots of therapy he would at least have a chance of leading a normal life.

Feeling hopeful, I turned around and gave Bran a stiff smile. "I love you," I assured him.

"I love you, too, Mommy," he replied, and then winked at me.

In that moment, he looked uncannily like Winking Walter, and a chill ran down my spine. I wondered if motherly love and intense therapy were enough to alter the behavior of someone who was genetically wired to be corrupt.

With a shaky hand, I tapped the screen of the navigation system, inputting the information for our next destination. Gripping the steering wheel, I took a deep breath before heading for the interstate highway.

About the Author

Aria Johnson is from Atlanta, GA. She grew up reading Mary Higgins Clark and Danielle Steele, Sidney Sheldon and other masters of thrillers and love. She always dreamed of writing spellbinding stories in which nothing is what it seems. Aria is hard at work on her next novel in her home office overlooking a dense forest.